THE DOG PARK IS BUNNY FREE.
FOR NOW.

"Look, ladies, I don't want to brag," I say. "But I have a certain amount of expertise when it comes to pests. My squirrel-chasing skills are legendary."

"That's for sure," Goldie cuts in.

"The bunnies clearly operate the same as squirrels. In evil gangs. Once word gets out that we have one of them . . . if the news hasn't gotten out already"— I shoot a quick peek at the back fence before going on—"the rest of the gang will surely try to chase us away and rescue him. They've already scared off the neighbors!"

"You sound awfully certain about that," Patches says.

"I saw it with my own eyes!" My tail rises with the realization. "I'll bet the one Hattie captured is their leader!"

Patches tilts her head in disbelief.

"It's the only thing that makes sense," I say. "Hattie calls him a strange word—*Thumper.* That must mean *Leader of the Evil Bunny Gang.*"

OTHER BOOKS YOU MAY ENJOY

Fenway and Hattie* and the Evil Bunny Gang

Victoria J. Coe

PUFFIN BOOKS

PUFFIN BOOKS
An imprint of Penguin Random House LLC
375 Hudson Street
New York, New York 10014

First published in the United States of America by G. P. Putnam's Sons,
an imprint of Penguin Random House LLC, 2017
Published by Puffin Books, an imprint of Penguin Random House LLC, 2018

THE LIBRARY OF CONGRESS HAS CATALOGED THE G. P. PUTNAM'S SONS EDITION AS FOLLOWS:
Names: Coe, Victoria J.
Title: Fenway and Hattie and the Evil Bunny Gang / Victoria J. Coe.
Description: New York, NY : G. P. Putnam's Sons, [2017]
Summary: "When Fenway's beloved short human, Hattie, brings home a
rival pet in the form of a fluffy, twitching rabbit, Fenway's determined to
oust the intruder—but doing so will cost him"—Provided by publisher.
Identifiers: LCCN 2016009820 | ISBN 9781101996331 (hardback)
Subjects: | CYAC: Jack Russell terrier—Fiction. | Dogs—Fiction. | Rabbits—
Fiction. | Pets—Fiction. | Human-animal relationships—Fiction. | BISAC:
JUVENILE FICTION / Animals / Dogs. | JUVENILE FICTION / Humorous
Stories. | JUVENILE FICTION / Lifestyles / Country Life.
Classification: LCC PZ7.1.C635 Fg 2017 | DDC [Fic]—dc23
LC record available at https://lccn.loc.gov/2016009820

Puffin Books ISBN 9781101996348

Design by Ryan Thomann and Dave Kopka
Printed in the United States of America

1 3 5 7 9 10 8 6 4 2

To Laurie and Matthew—
the Best Siblings Ever

CHAPTER 1

I'm out in the Dog Park behind our new house, enjoying a refreshing roll-around in the grass when I pick up the despicable smell of rodent. It can only be one thing—a squirrel!

Before I can react, Hattie flops down beside me. "Aw, Fenway," she coos, squinting at me in the bright sun.

I shimmy up to her till we're nose to nose. I give hers a sloppy lick. She tastes like the maple-y pancakes we shared this morning.

She giggles, stroking my fur the way she does at bedtime. What can I say? Hattie loves me more than anything in the whole world.

I go to snuggle her neck when that squirrel-y odor assaults my nose again. Stronger this time. That nasty rodent is way too close to my short human!

Don't they ever learn? I spring up, my hackles on high alert. I scan the porch, the bushes, the giant tree . . . aha! Over by the back fence, a flicker of movement. A flouncy tail. A chippery, chattery squawk. It's a nasty squirrel all right! I'm after him in a flash.

"Go away, Intruder!" I bark. "Can't you see the fence?"

He's not supposed to be here! Dog Parks are for dogs to play chase. And for Hattie to play ball with other short humans or Fetch Man. Even Food Lady's been playing in the Dog Park lately, digging in the dirt and sprinkling water in the patch where vegetables started growing.

Clearly, the Dog Park is no place for squirrels!

And this nasty squirrel is perched on a root of the giant tree, calmly swishing his tail like he's not in any danger at all. Is he really not intimidated by a ferocious Jack Russell Terrier? Or have his eyes and ears stopped working?

I snarl my fiercest snarl. "This is your last chance!"

Just as I'm ready to lunge, he shoots off the tree root and into the rustling bushes.

Does he think he can hide?

"I warned you! Now pay the consequences!" I plunge my snout in after him. That squirrel-y stench is almost unbearable.

I'm about to crawl under the bush when I hear *swish, snap* to my right.

His beady little head pops out of the next bush over. His body spurts out onto the grass, his fluffy tail whooshing behind him.

Panting wildly, I chase him through the grass. My sides are heaving, but I will not give up! I'm gaining on him! I'm about to grab his flouncy little tail—

But that nasty squirrel hurls himself onto the side fence. He scurries to the top and dives into the Dog Park next door.

"And don't come back!" I thrust out my chest in victory. Ridding the Dog Park of squirrels is a tough job. But luckily, I'm a professional.

I rush back to Hattie, who's headed toward the porch. I jump on her legs. "Great news!" I bark. "The nasty squirrel is gone."

She scoops me into her arms, showering me with kisses. She must be awfully grateful I saved her from the dangerous threat. Again.

"No big deal. Just doing my job," I bark, snuggling into her shirt.

Hattie hurries up the porch steps, happily hopping over a tangled jump rope, stepping around a rumpled sweatshirt, and kicking aside some old sneakers. The porch is good and messy, just the way Hattie likes it. Good thing Food Lady's not out here to ruin it.

"That squirrel put up a good fight, but he's no match for me." I nuzzle in for more kisses of appreciation.

But Hattie's got something else on her mind. She sets me down and snatches the fat leathery glove off the table. She pulls out a white ball and tosses it high above her head. She spins around as it shoots way up, then falls way down and lands—*thwap!*—inside the glove.

I squirm wildly with an awesome realization: We've got a ball to play with! I chase Hattie off the porch and back onto the grass.

"Yippee! Time to play," I bark, romping around her legs.

Hattie laughs and goes into her windup. I'm trotting out for a head start when we hear promising sounds from the Dog Park next door. *F-f-f-f-t!* A screen door sliding open . . . short human footsteps . . . and jingling dog tags!

"More great news, Hattie!" I bark, my tail thumping wildly. "Our best friends are coming!"

We head to the side fence and pause at our favorite spot—the new gate that appeared after Fetch Man and Tool Man spent a whole day banging and sawing. Now our Dog Park's even more fun than the big one back in the city, because we can romp around with our friends anytime we want.

Hattie's bouncing. I'm leaping and twirling. Because the Friend Gate is swinging open!

Out rushes a short human with a cap and a bushy tail of hair like Hattie's. It's our friend Angel!

"I'm so happy to see you," I bark, jumping on her dirt-smeared legs.

"Fenway, off!" Hattie commands.

I drop down, and Angel gives me a quick pat. She smells very excited. She waves her fat leathery glove at Hattie. She must really want to play.

A Golden Retriever and a white dog with black patches burst through the gate. Hooray! Hooray! It's Goldie and Patches!

We do the bum-sniffing circle dance. "'Sup, ladies?" I say, my tail swishing out of control.

"Something's gotten into our Angel," Goldie announces, tough and gruff as usual. "She's been buzzing around like a bee ever since breakfast."

"Actually, it started last night when she opened that envelope," Patches corrects in her lovely and gentle voice. "She practically exploded with glee."

Goldie shoots Patches a grumpy look. "The point is she's almost as energetic as Fenway. Just look at her."

Beaming, Angel unzips her jacket and twirls

around. It flaps in the warm breeze. Hattie looks on, impressed.

Wait a minute! Angel's wearing a jacket? Hattie hasn't worn a jacket in a Long, Long Time. She only wears jackets when it's cold or raining, not when it's hot and dry. Angel smooths the swishy jacket lovingly with her hands. She's acting awfully proud of it, even though one whiff reveals it's brand-new and hasn't ever been worn before.

Her eyes full of excitement, Angel reaches into the pocket and whips out two stiff, papery strips. She waves them in front of Hattie like they're a couple of bones. Or yummy hot dogs. Her face is glowing. I hear her exclaim two thrilling words that I know: "Fenway" and "park"!

My ears shoot up. Angel's talking about me!

Hattie pumps her fist in the air. "Yes! Yes! Yes!" she squeals.

I romp over to Angel. "Wowee! Are we going to the park?" I bark, my tail going nuts.

But Angel ignores me. Hattie, too. They leap up and slap hands. Then they start tossing the white ball back and forth.

I cock my head. We're not going anywhere. Didn't Angel say we were going to the park?

I look over at the ladies. And not a moment too soon.

Goldie's found a stick. She waggles it a few times, then takes off.

Talk about an irresistible invitation!

Me and Patches bolt across the grass. The chase is on!

Angel and Hattie are running around, too. The ball flies from one short human to the other. *Whizzzzz . . . thwap! Whizzzzz . . . thwap!* "Yeah!" Angel cries. She pulls the ball out of her glove and sends it back to Hattie.

Goldie rounds the giant tree near the back fence. Me and Patches are right on her tail, our tongues lolling, our sides heaving. We're so close to nabbing that stick!

"Careful, Fenway," Patches calls, panting. Angel's backpedaling right into our path. We weave around her in the nick of time.

That's Patches, always looking out for me. "Thanks," I cry.

"Fenway! Oh, Fenwaaaay!" Goldie's stopped near the side fence. Her eyes smug and taunting, she hovers over the stick. Which is lying still in the grass. And up for grabs.

It's too tempting to resist! Me and Patches tear after it. "That stick is mine!" I shout. My jaws are ready to chomp!

But at the very last second, Goldie snatches it and takes off the other way.

"No fair!" I yell. We sprint after her. I sneak a glance at Patches, who starts gaining ground on Goldie. She's going to beat me! There's only one thing to do—change my strategy.

Up ahead, I see the Best Idea Ever. Instead of making a wide turn, I take a shortcut through the vegetable patch.

I bound into the lettuce leaves, ready to tear on through. But I'm barely halfway across when I stop still in my tracks. Eeeeew, what's that horrible smell?

I take a look around. The soil isn't level and smooth the way it usually is. It's all dug up. The lettuces are toppled and torn. Uh-oh! Yesterday, they were full and leafy. Clearly, something is wrong.

Everywhere I look, there's more damage. A curly squash vine is severed, and its blossoms are gone. What's happened?

I sniff all around, my fur prickling with alarm. That scent is awfully mysterious! It's not a squirrel. Or a chipmunk. Or a bird. But it's a wild creature all right.

A sure sign of danger! I must discover who ruined the plants!

My nose follows the trail through fallen tomato stems and chewed pepper leaves to the most odorous spots. I plunge my snout into hole after hole, gathering news. Right away, I detect that the mysterious creature was here very recently. My fur prickles some more. What if he's lurking nearby, about to strike?

"Hey!" Hattie yells. Her arms flail as the white ball sails way over her head. She watches the ball land— *plop!*—right next to me, her eyes widening in horror. She's obviously alarmed by the terrible danger, too.

Like there's not a professional already on the case! "Don't worry, Hattie!" I bark, rummaging through the raggedy leaves. "I've got this!"

But as I'm crawling over a zucchini flower, my hind leg snags on a vine. The back door flies open and Food Lady races out.

@HapteR 2

"Hattie!" Food Lady sounds upset. She sprints across the porch, nearly tripping over Hattie's tangled jump rope.

"FEN-way!" Hattie cries, her voice high with alarm. She charges at me, right toward the danger!

I free my hind leg and dart around the ripped zucchini leaves. That nasty creature could still be at large. Anything could happen! "Nobody panic. I'll find the troublemaker!" I get back to sniffing like crazy.

Food Lady speeds through the grass. "FEN-way!" she snaps. Her arms wave. Her eyes bulge. She's clearly even more upset by the danger than Hattie is.

Hattie circles the vegetable patch, her arms reaching for me. "Fenway! Come!" she cries.

I scoot through the uneven soil, carefully avoiding

the holes. It's obvious Hattie and Food Lady want to help. But this job is way too dangerous for my humans. Especially when they're totally freaked out.

I must concentrate! I'm pawing around a tangle of squash vines where the mysterious stench is unmistakable when I see Food Lady's reaching fingers. She's always taking care of the vegetable patch. Nobody loves it as much as she does. Though she has to realize there's a professional right here, already hard at work.

I zoom deeper into the plants, my nose sniffing away. I must find the culprit and save the day!

Food Lady gasps and inspects the torn lettuce leaves. They look like they've been shredded. Or nibbled. It almost could be a clue. But who would destroy plants that smell like boring vegetables?

"I can hardly stand to watch," I hear Patches's lovely voice say.

"When will the guy ever learn?" Goldie murmurs.

It's nice to know the ladies appreciate the danger I'm in, but I think I can handle myself. Plus, I can't be distracted by my friends. Or a couple of fallen squash blossoms. The real evidence is right here in the dirt. And I'm going to find it. If I can just get to the right place to sniff . . .

I follow the scent to some stinky pellets. Aha! The evil creature's droppings? They sure smell suspicious.

And dropping-ish. Talk about promising! This could be the Greatest Discovery Yet. I must get a better sniff—hey!

Hattie clutches my collar and hoists me up. "FEN-way," she scolds. She avoids Food Lady's scowl.

I squirm. I kick. I must get loose! "Not now, Hattie! I have a job to do!"

Hattie doesn't seem to understand the danger we're in. Or how close I am to nabbing the culprit. She clutches me tighter.

Food Lady rises and shakes her head, her face frowning. She points at the torn plants, the ripped-up soil, then at us. She speaks with lots of words I don't know. "Wah-chim," she says. Her voice sounds accusing. Is she mad that Hattie interrupted my work? It's almost as if she's blaming us for the damage to the vegetables. Talk about a mix-up!

Hattie nods, her shoulders slumping. She winces at Food Lady but somehow manages to look hopeful at the same time. She glances at Angel, who reaches into her jacket and shows Food Lady the stiff, papery strips.

Hattie begs at Food Lady for a Long, Long Time. She says the same two thrilling words that Angel did: "Fenway" and "park." She tilts her head. "Please? Please? Please?"

My tail thumps. Hattie wants to take me to the park!

But Food Lady is not so sure. She crosses her arms and lets out a whooshy breath. She goes back to talking in that exasperated tone. She points at the porch littered with Hattie's things. She points at the raggedy plants. She points at me, kicking wildly in Hattie's arms.

Hattie's eyes are still pleading. Her words come out quickly, and her voice sounds desperate. She smells impatient. And determined.

Food Lady raises an eyebrow.

Hattie sucks in a breath. She exchanges a questioning glance with Angel. The short humans clearly want to get back to playing ball instead of listening to Food Lady being angry.

I know how they feel. I wiggle harder. If only I could convince Hattie to put me down. I have to get back to that vegetable patch and keep investigating. The clues are in there!

While Hattie and Food Lady talk some more, Angel quietly takes the glove off her hand. She trudges toward the Friend Gate, gesturing for Goldie and Patches to follow. Before shutting the gate, Angel sneaks a glance back at Hattie. Her eyes are hopeful, her thumbs up.

"See you later, Fenway," Patches mutters.

When everybody's gone, Food Lady points again at the dug-up soil, the ripped-up vegetables, the porch where Hattie's clothes and sneakers and toys are strewn all over. She crosses her arms.

Hattie gets back to begging. "Please-please-please," she says.

Food Lady's face softens. She must be starting to cave because she lets out a sigh and says, "Weul-see."

"Yes!" Claiming victory, Hattie sets me down. She kneels beside a toppled tomato stem and begins heaping dirt around it.

Finally, I can get back to work! I immediately crawl through the dug-up soil, sniffing and pawing for clues. That creature cannot have gone far!

"Fenway!" Food Lady shrieks, rushing at me.

Before I can even pick up the trail, Hattie's hands close around me. Hey, I barely got started!

Food Lady frowns at the vegetable patch. She frowns at us. She points back at the house.

Her shoulders sunk, Hattie carries me up the porch steps to the sliding door. When we get inside, she tosses the ball and glove on a chair and grabs my leash.

On cue, my tail comes to life, but then quickly droops. The leash means we're going for a walk. But how can we walk at a time like this? There's terrible danger happening in the Dog Park. I have to save my family from evil! This is a disaster!

The instant Hattie puts me down, I hustle to the back

door. "We can't leave the Dog Park," I bark. "There's too much at stake!"

Obviously, she doesn't get it. She drags me through the house and out the front door. Despite my very clear protests, she's evidently decided to go for a walk no matter what.

Or maybe not? Hattie flops down in the middle of the lawn. With apparently no intention of moving. Or doing anything at all.

What—are we supposed to just sit here and do nothing?

Or could her laziness mean opportunity? I try to tug her toward the driveway. How easy would it be to go around the garage and through the side gate? "Come on, Hattie," I bark. "We need to get back to the Dog Park."

"Fenway, stay," she commands, yanking on my leash.

I plop next to her, studying her stubborn face. There's some mysterious reason she won't let me go. But what is it?

And she seems angry at me, too. Hey, it's not my fault I couldn't do my job. It's the very definition of frustrating. I'm supposed to be tracking down a monster, probably a violent criminal, and I'm stuck here in the front yard.

I'm sinking back down in the grass when I realize

maybe there is something I can do. I drop my nose to the ground and sniff. Clues could be anywhere!

I scout around, picking up only boring weeds and pesky chipmunks and the same random birds I always smell. I lift my head and listen. But all I hear is a motor buzzing in the distance. There are no signs of trouble. My tail sags with the horrible realization.

There isn't anything I can do.

Hattie's sagging, too. Her chin sinks into her hands. Maybe she's mad that we couldn't keep playing in the Dog Park. We were all having so much fun until that nasty creature ruined everything! And he's probably ready to strike again!

I gaze up at Hattie's frowning face. I remember my other important job.

"Cheer up, Hattie," I bark, nuzzling her leg. "Your best buddy is here."

She gives me a quick pat. But she still smells angry.

Clearly, she needs more convincing. I hop onto her lap and lick her cheek. "Even though bad things are happening, we've got each other," I bark. "That's all that matters."

Hattie cups her hand behind my head. Staring into my eyes, she speaks in a low and serious voice. "Bee-have," she says over and over.

When she's done speaking, I snuggle against her

neck. I smell her bad feelings start to fade away. Whoopee! I knew I could cheer her up.

As Hattie scratches my ears, she glances over at Angel's house next door. She looks back at me and whispers, "Fenway, park," clearly filling me in on a plan. Or a secret. Even though she's whispering, she sounds forceful, sure. As if her mind is made up and it's not going to change.

Hooray! Hooray! We're going to the park! I spring up, pulling her toward the driveway again. But she doesn't budge. Maybe we're going to the park later?

I curl up in Hattie's lap for a while, watching a fluttery butterfly. The occasional car zooming down the street. A boy short human riding a bicycle.

At last, when it seems like nothing interesting will happen, a car slows and turns into the driveway across the street. When the doors open, my ears perk.

A tall human gets out of one side of the car and heads toward the mailbox. A lady human takes her time getting out of the other side.

Hattie's eyes widen. She jolts up. She smells excited, like she's gotten an idea. She leads me to the edge of the yard, her head swiveling from one end of the street to the other.

Are we finally going for a walk?

Apparently not. We race toward the tall humans, Hattie shouting friendly greetings.

The man smiles and tucks a rolled-up newspaper under his arm. The lady turns, one arm waving, the other behind her back.

As we approach, I get busy sizing up the tall humans. The man is wearing glasses and has dark whiskers on his jaw. The lady has a belly so big and round, she wobbles a little like she might topple over. They look just like our neighbors, Whisker Face and Round Lady. But smelling is believing.

I zoom in on their shoes, my nose going wild. *Sniff, sniff* . . . the lady smells like pickles and vanilla ice cream. The man smells like paint and new carpeting. And a mysterious animal scent that's very familiar.

Yippee! It really is Whisker Face and Round Lady. I jump on their legs. "I'm so glad to see you!" I bark.

Whisker Face rubs my head. "Aw, Fenway," he says. Round Lady tries to stoop down, too, but groans like the effort is too much.

"Are we here for a barbecue again?" I paw Whisker Face's leg. "I love barbecues!" I sniff more of his friendly aroma. There's always been something mysterious about it that I can't quite identify. Sort of furry. And unpleasant . . .

"Fenway, off!" Hattie commands.

I plop onto my bum.

"Good boy," Hattie says, beaming with pride.

The neighbors exchange looks, obviously impressed.

Hattie asks them questions. Her voice is excited.

Round Lady smiles and pats her big belly. "Sooooon," she croons.

Whisker Face pets my head again. I sniff his legs some more. That mysterious animal scent reminds me of something . . . hey! It's like that stench from the vegetable patch.

My fur bristles. This is it! The clue I've been after!

CHAPTER 3

My nose goes into overdrive. I sniff
Whisker Face's sneakers, his ankles, every hair on his
legs. The scent is a lot like that evil creature who caused
all the trouble in the vegetable patch. But not exactly
the same. Another evil creature? His brother? Cousin?
There's definitely a connection. And it's full of mystery!

One thing's for sure—there's more than one of
those creatures lurking around. Some sort of evil gang!
I knew there was danger. Good thing I'm on the case!

I move on to Round Lady's feet. Sure enough, she's
covered with the exact same mysterious scent as Whisker

Face. I'm definitely on to something! My nose more sure than ever, I jump wildly, sniffing Round Lady's calves all the way up to the hem of her dress.

"Fenway!" Hattie scoops me into her arms. She strokes my back, clearly encouraging my efforts.

"Thanks!" I bark, and I didn't even ask for help. Now that I'm up higher, I thrust my snout into Round Lady's chest.

Hattie pulls me away from the target. She makes a sorry face at the neighbors, but they just exchange glances and smile.

"I thought you were trying to help, Hattie," I bark. "I can't do my job from a distance!" I point my snout at Round Lady and inhale as hard as I can. Even from here, that odor is unmistakable.

As usual, Hattie is completely unaware of the problem. She continues chatting with Whisker Face and Round Lady like nothing is wrong. Actually, she sounds like everything is suddenly right. Hattie speaks with a very excited voice. A grin spreads across her face. "Thumper?" she asks, then points to herself. "Wah-chim?"

Round Lady raises her eyebrows in surprise. She gazes expectantly at Whisker Face and pats her belly again.

I poke my nose out as far as I can, sniffing with all

my might. But it's no use. I'm too far away to crack that unpleasant animal-ish smell. When there are two evil creatures, there are always more! Obviously, with a new gang roaming around the neighborhood, it's only a matter of time before they cause more trouble. Or worse, take over! They must be stopped.

But first, they must be found. I wiggle furiously in Hattie's arms. I'm desperate to get loose, but she only grabs me tighter. "FEN-way," she scolds.

"Hattie, you don't understand," I bark. "This is an emergency!" I twist. I turn. I thrust my snout at Whisker Face and Round Lady.

Hattie tightens her grip even more. "Look!" she says to the neighbors. Her voice sounds like she's reassuring them about something. Then she turns to me. "Fenway, leave it!" she commands.

My head snaps back to her. I stop twisting and sniffing. Why'd she pick a time like this to play the leave-it game?

Whisker Face and Round Lady look impressed. They share a questioning glance, then shrug.

"Okay," Whisker Face says to Hattie.

"Yes!" she cries, pumping her fist. She and the neighbors chatter for a while longer. Hattie nods her head so much, I'm wondering if she'll ever stop.

Eventually, the neighbors turn to go. They head up their walkway and disappear inside the front door, taking their scents with them!

I crawl up Hattie's shoulder, watching them go. She strokes my neck, all calm and soothing. Clearly, I'm going to have to work a lot harder to uncover the evil gang's plot.

As we hurry across the street to our house, I catch sight of a short human rushing toward us. Silky black hair hangs over one shoulder, and her white skirt puffs out behind her. A grin sweeps over her face. She's clutching a box that rattles with every step. "Hattie!" she calls.

"Zahra!" Hattie cries.

The instant Zahra reaches us, she leans in and smothers me with kisses. "Awww, Fenway," she coos, giggling.

Yippee! I love Zahra! I lick her chin. She smells like glitter and glue. Just like the sparkly bracelets up and down her arm.

Hattie gazes at the bracelets. "Oooooh," she says, her voice filled with admiration.

Zahra pats the rattly box, her cheeks smiling even harder than before.

Hattie claps her hands, and we all race up to the

front door. When we get inside, Hattie finally sets me down. At last, I can get back to work!

I speed through the hall to the back door. Maybe I missed my chance to sniff out the clues on the neighbors, but I can always get back to the original source of the trouble—the vegetable patch.

"Somebody let me out!" I bark, scratching the screen.

"FEN-way!" Hattie shouts. She snatches me up and looks nervously out into the Dog Park.

Food Lady pops up from behind the leafy lettuce plants. She wipes her brow. Her face is scowling.

"Uh-oh." Hattie glances at Zahra, her shoulders slumping. She smells worried. She must realize it's not safe to go back into the Dog Park.

"It's dangerous all right," I bark, licking her cheek. "But I can protect you."

Instead of being reassured, Hattie turns away.

I squirm wildly. "I have to get out there and track that evil creature," I bark. But it's no use. We bound up the stairs, Hattie hugging me tight. It's clear she's not getting the message. But as we dash into her room, I get a new idea.

I shoot out of Hattie's arms and up onto the bed. My paws rest on the window ledge. I peer through the screen, scanning the Dog Park for clues.

Food Lady is squatting next to the vegetables, her hands busy in the dirt. She looks serious. Focused. And unsuspecting.

My hackles shoot up. Could she be the evil creature's next target?

I redouble my efforts, examining the whole area. If he's lurking around somewhere, I'll spot him.

My gaze wanders to the Dog Park next door. There's no sign of the villain over there, either. Angel is tossing a white ball up in the air and catching it in her glove. Goldie is snoozing on the porch. Patches is sprawled out in the grass, halfheartedly gnawing on a bone. They're all together, but each one looks bored and lonely. And even worse, the Friend Gate is shut.

This is not how it's supposed to be. We were all outside having fun before that evil creature ruined the vegetable patch and got Food Lady all upset. I drop onto the bed in disgust.

Zahra plops down beside me and opens her box. Out spill rattly beads, floppy bands, and shiny clasps. Hattie's eyes get wide. She smells excited.

Zahra starts stringing beads and looping bands. Pretty soon, she's got a glimmer-y rope that looks like half a bracelet. She shows it to Hattie, who claps her hands.

As Zahra gets back to work, Hattie lifts me onto her lap and rubs my neck.

Ah, right there. That's the spot. I roll onto my back so the belly scratching can begin. My hind leg kicks with delight.

Now Zahra's holding up a sparkly bracelet just like the ones on her arm. Her face is triumphant. She wraps the new bracelet around Hattie's wrist.

Hattie's eyes widen. "Oooooh," she says, her voice full of gratitude.

I pop up and give it a sniff. It smells like plastic. I curl up tighter in Hattie's cozy lap while she starts stringing and looping like Zahra did. Next thing I know, a bumpy new collar winds around my neck. Hattie gazes into my eyes and pats my head.

Awww . . . she's the best short human ever.

Later, my whole family—Fetch Man, Food Lady, and Hattie—gathers around the table in the Eating Place like they do every night. I'm perched next to Hattie's chair, ready for delicious drips or tasty morsels to fall. The Eating Place smells like wonderful spaghetti and meatballs. My tummy is grumbling. My tongue is drooling.

The humans are chattering as always. But tonight, everyone's attention is focused on Fetch Man. Hattie says two words, "Fenway" and "park," over and over, her voice full of enthusiasm. She's obviously telling him about the secret plan.

"Wow! Whoa!" Fetch Man cries. He is clearly just as enthusiastic as she is.

I pant with anticipation. It's a pretty exciting plan! I can hardly wait to go to the park! It's probably the Best Park Ever, with loads of cool friends and lots of grass to chase them around in. And maybe even hot dogs!

But nobody is getting up and grabbing the leash. They just keep sitting there. Hattie is so busy chattering and Fetch Man is so busy listening that they don't even acknowledge me. Hattie must be talking about Angel next because she says her name a bunch of times, her legs jiggling, her arms gesturing. Finally, she takes a deep breath. "Can-I-can-I . . . ?" she begs.

Fetch Man turns to Food Lady, who's speaking to him in an exasperated voice. She says my name a bunch of times. She does not say "park." But she does say "rect" and "gar-din."

When Food Lady stops talking, Fetch Man turns to Hattie and shrugs. His face is pained. "Bee-riss-pon-si-bull?" he asks.

That must mean something really exciting, because Hattie almost bounces out of her seat. "I will! I will!" she cries.

Food Lady looks skeptical. "Wah-chim," she says. Then, "Weul-see."

Hattie shifts in her seat. She smells disappointed, like she's losing a battle over a bone. But her body language says she's not ready to give up. There's still some fight left in her. She crosses her fingers under the table. I give them a lick. They taste like garlic.

Hattie sits up tall. "Thum-per," she says. She keeps on chattering, her voice sounding strong. Like she's boasting. She taps her chest and adds, "Wah-chim."

Fetch Man looks skeptical. Food Lady glances down at me, then back at Hattie. "Wah-chim-too?" she asks.

Hattie nods vigorously. "I-can-I-can," she says, full of determination. And then, "Fenway, park?"

My tail swishes hopefully. Is it time to go?

Fetch Man and Food Lady exchange questioning eyebrows. "Weul-see," Food Lady says again. Hattie reaches down and gives me a pat of encouragement. I think she is telling me to be patient about the park.

After supper, Hattie rushes from the table, leaving Food Lady alone with sudsy dishes in the sink. I get busy chomping delicious kibble, vaguely aware of Fetch Man quietly ducking into the garage.

Upstairs, I cuddle in Hattie's bed. She kisses my brown paw, then the white one. She nuzzles her nose in my fur. "Best buddies, best buddies," she sings, running the brush through my coat. Her voice is low and quiet.

The light goes out and I close my eyes . . .

I'm all alone out in the Dog Park, walking through the vegetable patch. One moment the plants are strong and leafy, then poof! *They're toppled and broken and ripped to shreds. Obviously, the work of monsters! They must be stopped.*

I find tracks in the mud. A clue!

I'm hot on the trail, panting and eager. I spot something I hadn't noticed before.

Evil Creatures. Everywhere I turn! Under the bushes. In the grass. On the fence.

I'm completely surrounded. And I can't take my eyes off them.

They look like squirrels, only fatter and uglier.

And gigantic.

Their fangs are dripping with viciousness. Their claws are jagged and ready to strike!

"G-g-go away, you n-n-nasty creatures." I sink under a floppy leaf, my whole body trembling. "Or else."

Then, out of nowhere, Hattie appears! She's climbing down the giant tree trunk—from her little house up in the branches.

"No! Hattie!" I bark. "It's not safe!"

The Evil Creatures roar with laughter. Before I can move, they close in. And seize her.

CHAPTER 4

My eyes open to morning sunshine.
Dazzling light dances on top of the dresser—all around
Hattie's bracelet.

I remember Zahra and the sparkly beads, the chewed-
up garden, the Gigantic Evil Creatures! Shuddering, I
search for Hattie.

Great news! She's not gone! Her sleepy head is resting
on her pillow. For now.

I lick Hattie awake. "There's danger outside," I bark,
my tail raised in alarm. "I have to investigate!"

She nuzzles my nose and strokes my neck.

I drop down and give the bumpy new collar a scratch.
It sure is itchy.

Hattie hops out of bed and chases me downstairs.

Food Lady's on her knees surrounded by strong-smelling cleaners.

Hattie heads to the back door. As soon as she slides it open, I shoot into the Dog Park. Hey, it's empty. Except for a buzzing bee. And a bobbing robin. A few strategic sniffs confirm it's all clear on the squirrel front. And other evil creatures in general.

Talk about a relief! I turn around. Where's Hattie?

I peer through the screen door, but her bare feet have disappeared. At least she's safe inside. And besides, I have work to do.

I sniff for the familiar spot and get busy watering the bushes. And then I notice something new.

My nose on high alert, I trot over to check it out. The vegetable patch is surrounded by a wobbly wire fence. It's lower than a regular fence, but it's too high for me to jump over. What's it doing here? And how am I supposed to get in and check for evidence?

I'm sniffing the perimeter and detecting the work of Fetch Man when I stop dead in my tracks. The horrible stench. A pile of droppings like before. Only fresher. And more of them.

This can only mean one thing—the mysterious creature has come back. With reinforcements!

My ears fall. I cower against the wire fence. My

head swivels. The picture is coming into focus. My suspicions were right!

The monster who ripped up the vegetable patch. His friends. And his brother or cousin across the street. They're definitely a gang! I'll bet there are even more of them—swarming everywhere, planning their next attack!

I creep out into the grass, my hackles raised, my eyes peeled. Besides the droppings, there's no sign of them. Or is there?

I pick up a suspicious odor nearby. Nose to the ground, I follow the trail across the whole Dog Park, over the giant tree root, and all the way to the back fence.

What's this?

Somebody dug a hole under the fence. And not just a hole—a tunnel! I paw the loose soil. One sniff confirms what I already know. It's the gang's dirty work all right!

I must investigate. The tunnel is probably dangerous. And it's clearly too small to crawl through.

But I have to uncover their plot. There's too much at stake. I have to protect Hattie. I'm a professional!

I drop to my belly and jab my snout under the fence. The stench is stronger than ever. I shimmy. I push. My head squeezes through the hole . . .

And I'm peeking into another open space, with grass and trees and a big house at one end. My nostrils are sniffing, my ears are straining, my eyes are searching—

Hey! A pair of hands pulls me back into the Dog Park. "Hattie! What are you thinking?" I bark, kicking in protest. "I was about to find the dangerous villains!"

She hugs me tight. Her eyes gawk like she's never seen a hole before. She glances back at the house, smelling worried, her heart thudding in her chest. She turns to me, her brow wrinkled. "FEN-way," she scolds. "Bee-have."

She kneels down and lets me go with a sigh. Then she starts shoving dirt into the hole as fast as she can.

Uh-oh! If that hole's filled in, how can I get through and nab the gang? I must stop her!

As soon as Hattie steps away, my paws get digging. I have to undo the damage!

"No!" she cries, shooing me to the side. Doesn't she realize this is the danger spot? The source of all the trouble?

She pushes me to the side again, then rushes around gathering rocks and twigs. This is not the time for a game of fetch.

"We can play later, Hattie," I bark. "After I save us from sure disaster!"

Apparently, she can't wait. She collects more dirt

and rocks and sticks. She feverishly stuffs them into the hole.

I race around her feet. "What have you done? That hole is the key to my entire strategy!"

Just then, the Friend Gate creaks open, and we both turn. Angel dashes through. Followed by Goldie and Patches. My own reinforcements!

I rush over to greet them, my tail wagging wildly.

Angel's jacket flaps as she runs. Her cap is on her head. Her fat leathery glove is on one hand. The other one's clutching the white ball. How can she think of playing when danger is so close?

Goldie and Patches scamper over, tails twirling, tags jingling.

"Ladies! Am I ever glad you're here," I say as we do the bum-sniffing circle dance.

Patches cocks her head. "Is something up?"

Goldie looks curious.

"The Biggest Something Ever!" I lead them straight to the back fence, where Hattie is crouching.

Angel comes up behind us, her eyebrows arched. "Fenway, park?" she asks anxiously.

My ears perk. Are we going to the park now?

Hattie springs up, chattering. "May-bee," she says, her voice sounding hopeful.

Angel doesn't look so sure. She gazes at the pile of dirt and rocks and sticks that Hattie made.

My ears droop.

"What's this?" Goldie asks, nosing around the back fence. "I don't remember this mound being here before."

"Remember the ruined vegetable patch?" I say. "It was the work of an evil creature."

"Really?" Patches sounds concerned.

"Get this," I say. "He's part of a gang. I found a tunnel under the fence." I nod at the used-to-be hole. "That's how they're infiltrating the Dog Park."

Patches looks impressed. "What a discovery!"

"For all the good it did me." My tail sinks. "Hattie filled it in. After I only got halfway through!"

Goldie gruffs. "You tried to squeeze through? Was that the smartest move? You could've been sprayed. Or attacked by spiky quills."

"Oh my!" Patches's eyes widen in alarm. "Do you think it was a skunk? Or a porcupine?"

"Well, I don't know," I say, horrible images flashing through my head. "They smell a bit squirrel-ish, but sort of like rotten vegetables, too. They're pure evil!"

Goldie and Patches exchange an awkward glance. "Squirrel-ish? Like rotten vegetables? Are you sure we're not talking about bunnies?" Goldie says, laughing. "Dangerous bunnies?"

Bunnies? Even the name reeks of Evil. I shudder.

"Do they have floppy ears and big teeth?" Patches asks me. "And fluffy cotton tails?"

Goldie shakes her head. "Bunnies aren't dangerous. What do they do, hop around? Nibble the plants? Leave a few droppings?"

The ladies obviously don't get it. They've never had to defend their short human from nasty squirrels or . . . *bunnies*, if that's what I'm up against. I watch my beloved Hattie rush to the porch for her leathery glove. I hang my head. "I can't let them take her."

"Don't worry, Fenway." Patches gives my neck a friendly nudge. "Nothing will ever—hey, is that a new collar?"

Goldie moves in for a closer look. "Are those beads? And sparkles?"

"Hattie made it," I say, dropping down for a quick scratch.

"How lovely," Patches says.

"It's not really your style," Goldie huffs.

"What can I say? Hattie's always fussing over me," I say. "But why does that matter now? Evil Bunnies are about to strike! And they're probably on the other side of that fence right now." I charge in and get back to pawing the dirt.

"Evil Bunnies? About to strike?" Goldie says, peering over my shoulder. "Trust me, Fenway, all bunnies do is hop around. They're hardly worth the effort."

"And digging holes in the yard might not be such a good idea," Patches says.

I should've expected Goldie to be unconvinced, but Patches is usually on my side. Why isn't she at least supporting my cause? "I'll show you both!" I dig furiously through the dirt and rocks. I grab twig after twig. I have to keep at it! There's so much work to do!

But the ladies are really not getting it. "Besides, you're only making it easier for them to come in," Goldie sneers.

"And something bad might happen," Patches warns.

"Correction!" I shout between snatching twigs. "Something bad will definitely happen if I don't catch them!"

I'm pawing aside one of the last remaining rocks when the ladies suddenly back away. I hear footsteps coming up behind me. Food Lady gasps. "FEN-way!" she cries.

Huh? How long has she been there?

Food Lady scoops me up, smelling anything but

affectionate. "Hattie!" she shouts through clenched teeth.

"What?" Hattie calls from across the Dog Park as Angel snags the ball. When she sees Food Lady brushing the dirt off my snout, Hattie's expression plummets.

Chapter 5

I race around the Eating Place while Hattie finishes lunch. I'm way too wound up to sit beside her patiently waiting for crumbs. And for some reason she's acting annoyed. Well, that makes two of us! I'm pretty annoyed myself! Why did Food Lady have to come and interrupt my work? That Evil Bunny Gang is not going to defeat itself.

I head to the back door. "Come on, Hattie," I bark. I must return to that tunnel under the fence!

But when she finally gets up, Food Lady apparently has another idea. She hands Hattie my leash.

"A walk? But I have an important job to do," I bark in protest. It's no use. The next thing I know, the leash is hooked to my collar, and Hattie's leading me out the front door with a sigh.

Those Evil Bunnies are probably running rampant through the Dog Park at this very moment. They must be stopped.

I sniff every inch of the front walk. If bunnies are anywhere nearby, I'll find them. I zigzag through the grass while Hattie huffs and grunts and tugs the leash.

When we get to the street, Hattie turns. "Let's go, Fenway," she says. And even though we're getting farther and farther away from the clues, my tail starts wagging.

Because we're heading up the walkway to the house next door. The ladies' house. They weren't much help before, but maybe I can convince Goldie and Patches to help me figure out how to prevent the gang from taking over.

Angel and the ladies burst out the door. My tail whirls around and around. We go in for the sniff exchange.

As we trot toward the street, Hattie gestures at Whisker Face and Round Lady's house. "Thum-per . . . wah-chim," she says as she proudly points to her chest.

Angel's eyebrows arch.

Hattie chatters on excitedly, growing more and more confident. Like she's telling Angel about a foolproof plan. "Fenway, park," she says, her voice hopeful.

Wowee! Are we going to the special park now?

Angel gives her a smile of approval.

My tail begins to swish. But then it stops when I remember that I have trouble to deal with.

We head up the street, and Patches turns to me. "Why so serious, Fenway? We're going for a walk."

I can't really blame Patches for not understanding. She's way too nice. If she came nose to nose with an Evil Bunny, she'd probably welcome him like a new friend. I have to make them understand the very real threat. "I need to stop the Evil Bunny Gang," I say. "Before they ruin everything."

"Is it possible you're making too much of this?" Patches asks in her usual gentle tone. "I hear bunnies are pretty harmless."

We pause to sniff a tree that smells like the Schnauzer on the next block.

When we're done catching up on the news, Goldie gruffs. "Well, I suppose bunnies aren't *entirely* harmless." She snaps at a fly. "It certainly seems like one of them tore up that vegetable patch."

My fur bristles. "That's right!" At least Goldie's starting to see reason. Funny, she's normally the one who argues about everything. I sneak a glance at my beloved Hattie, strolling along, happy as can be. Completely unsuspecting. "And what if they—"

Hey, what's that? A stripy chipmunk scurries across my path. I lunge after it . . . until a sharp yank on my collar stops me short.

"Fenn-waay," Hattie coaxes.

As that stripy blur dives under a bush, all I can do is watch. "I'll get you next time!" I bark, then turn back to the ladies. "Now, where was I?"

"Evil Bunnies?" Goldie offers. "What if they . . . ?"

I sneak a look at my beloved Hattie again. "Those bunnies can't hurt her! I won't let them." I turn to Goldie, trembling. "I'm telling you! It's an emergency!" At least Goldie is beginning to get it. Why doesn't Patches sound convinced?

I'm about to press my case, but up ahead I spy another distraction. A short human is squatting at the end of a driveway. Golden sunlight sparkles off her headband, and dark silky hair hangs over one shoulder. Her hand moves purposefully on the pavement. Chalky pictures appear.

"Zahra," Hattie calls.

Yippee! I love Zahra! We hurry over, and I jump on her knees. "I'm so happy to see you," I bark.

Zahra laughs. "Fenn-waay!" she sings. She runs her fingers over my bumpy new collar, nodding her approval. She nuzzles my nose.

I lick her hand. It tastes like chalk.

Hattie peers at the pictures on the driveway where Zahra was crouching. "Oooooh," Hattie says, her voice filled with admiration.

Angel shrugs. Apparently she does not share Hattie's interest in the driveway. She must not be into the sparkly bracelets either, because she scowls at Zahra's arm like the glittering light is hurting her eyes.

Zahra doesn't seem to notice. She plucks pieces of chalk from a small box and offers them to the short humans. "Here!" she says, grinning.

Hattie grabs the chalk. "Cool!" she cries.

But Angel doesn't respond. Instead, she looks at me and the ladies. "C'mon," she says to Hattie.

Hattie sighs and gives the chalk back to Zahra, whose eyes look sad and disappointed. Then Hattie brightens and nudges Zahra's shoulder. "Go for a walk?" she asks.

Zahra springs up. "Okay!"

Angel offers a weak smile. She smells anxious.

Zahra dashes into the house, then pops right back out again. She skips to the end of the driveway, her puffy skirt bouncing. "Let's go!" she cries.

"How wonderful," Patches says as we all get back to walking. "Zahra is joining us."

"Zahra's awesome," I say, practically strutting as our whole pack heads down the street.

Hattie and Zahra chatter a lot while Zahra spins

her sparkly bracelets. Hattie gazes longingly at them, then glances at her own bare wrist like it's let her down somehow.

Angel looks away, frowning.

"I'm not impressed," says Goldie with a sneer. "She fusses over the new one and ignores the rest."

Patches shoots her a warning look. "Don't mind her," she says to me in her lovely voice. "Sometimes it's hard for her to forget the past."

Goldie glares. "Easy for you to say," she nearly growls. "You're not the one who was ignored for so long."

Patches rolls her eyes.

What are they going on about? And what does this have to do with anything? "Hey, ladies. Why all the grouching?" I say.

Goldie turns to me. "You don't know how great you've got it, Fenway. Enjoy being fussed over while it lasts."

I stop in my tracks. "What do you mean?"

"Don't mind her," Patches says. "Nothing will ever come between you and Hattie."

Come between us? Who said anything about that?

"Fenn-waay," Hattie coos, tugging at the leash.

I trot to catch up to the pack. "What could possibly come between me and Hattie?"

Goldie narrows her eyes.

"Like I said—nothing," Patches says kindly.

We pause at a tree for another newsy sniff. Apparently, a Poodle had hot dogs for breakfast. Talk about a juicy bit of information. We can hardly get enough.

Except for Goldie, who's not even sniffing that hard. She turns her back on the tree with a humph. Since when doesn't she love gossip?

At least the short humans are having a good time. Zahra caresses the sleeve of Angel's swooshy jacket, her eyes wide in awe.

Angel shrugs and smiles. For real this time. She chatters with Zahra in a proud voice.

Hattie gazes ahead happily. She links arms with the other two short humans, and we walk the rest of the way home.

Later, when our friends are gone, I rocket into the Dog Park. The walk was nice, but I have work to get back to. I sniff every blade of grass, every patch of soil. There's no time to waste.

I'm so busy sniffing, I can hardly think. It's not until I've covered the entire Dog Park that I finally realize how much the bunny stench has faded.

I sink down and scratch under my beady new collar. Has the Evil Bunny Gang given up? Have they found another short human to target?

It wouldn't be the first time I've scared off a bunch of evil creatures with my mere presence. What can I say? I can be pretty ferocious when I set my mind to it.

I spend the rest of the day relaxing. Who knew foiling Evil Bunnies would be so easy?

When Hattie calls me inside, I'm still congratulating myself on a job well done. She probably wants to give me a reward. Like maybe we're going to that park now!

I romp through the house, my tail going nuts. It's got to be the Best Park Ever. I'll bet there's a big field to run around in and balls to chase. And probably no squirrels!

But my tail sags when Hattie heads out the front door without me. "Bee-have," she warns, waving her finger before she disappears.

What's that about?

From the window above the couch, I watch her vanish into Whisker Face and Round Lady's house across the street. I wait and wait. At last, she reappears. Carrying a Very Large Cage.

Chapter 6

Hooray! Hooray! I rush to the door. Hattie was gone for so long and I missed her so much. I can't wait to play! My tail's swishing so hard, I nearly lose my balance.

But when she steps inside—*eeeee-yoooww!* I leap back, my nostrils shuddering at the all-too-familiar stench. It can only be one thing—an Evil Bunny!

Right here in our home! What can this mean? My fur stands up in protest.

Hattie carries the Very Large Cage into the Lounging Place as Fetch Man strides in. He does not smell the least bit surprised that an Evil Bunny has entered our home.

He clears piles of books and magazines off the low table as Food Lady comes over. She's wiping her hands on a dish towel. Her eyes are wide and curious, though she doesn't smell surprised, either. I sidle up beside them, my hackles raised.

Hattie sets the cage down, and we gather around to inspect her catch. She thrusts out her chest, proud and strong. For obvious reasons! But how did she nab this Evil Bunny? And does the rest of the gang know?

"Thum-per," Hattie announces, her face beaming. We all lean in for a peek.

The wire cage is half as long as the table. The bottom is stuffed with paper and hay. On the outside is a plastic bottle, and on the inside is a bowl. But that's not all.

Huddled in the corner farthest from us is a brown ball of fur. And based on the ladies' description, he's clearly an Evil Bunny and even worse than I imagined! With whiskers, long floppy ears, and big teeth. Not to mention a nose that's constantly twitching. His beady eyes are glaring, his wretched voice is growling, and his whole body reeks!

I take a few steps back, even though he's trapped and unable to attack. For now.

Hattie talks and talks, apparently explaining how she captured the Evil Bunny. Her voice is awfully excited.

Fetch Man and Food Lady exchange glances. He's nodding, but her eyebrows are questioning.

"Look," Hattie says. She pulls a piece of paper out of her pocket, unfolds it, and waves it at them. She holds it in front of her face and stares at it, her eyes darting from side to side. "Food . . . drink . . . clean-ing . . ." she says.

When Hattie finishes speaking, Food Lady crosses her arms, her head tilting in my direction. Fetch Man does the same thing. "Chores?" he asks, his voice skeptical. "And Fenway?"

Hattie hovers over me. Her expression is serious. "Fenway, sit," she commands.

I drop onto my bum, gazing up at her the way she likes.

"Good boy." She squats down to pat my head, and I lick her happy cheek.

Hattie rises, her hand held out toward me. "Stay," she demands. She takes a step back.

I gape at her like she's a piece of ripply bacon. When my beloved Hattie gives me that look, nothing can come between us.

"Good boy, Fenway!" She rushes over and wraps me in a hug.

Playing games with Hattie is my favorite thing to do. But isn't this a strange time for games? The Evil

Bunny is sitting right there on the low table, growling with wickedness. We need to remain on guard!

Hattie turns to Fetch Man and Food Lady. "See?" she says.

They exchange glances again. Their eyebrows are questioning.

"Watch!" Hattie scoops me up. She holds my nose frighteningly close to the cage. "Fenn-waay," she says in her sweetest voice. "Thum-per, Thum-per."

I flinch. What is she saying? And what is she trying to do? Torture me with bunny stench?

The Evil Bunny emits a deeper, more rumbly growl. He hasn't moved, but he's clearly up to no good.

"Best buddies," she coos, even though it's not night-time and she's not brushing me. But that's not the only thing that's wrong. Hattie reaches a finger into the cage and strokes the Evil Bunny's floppy ears. She couldn't be petting him. Could she?

The nasty fur ball's growling sounds different. Is he clicking or clacking? Or purring?

Whoa. Hattie must feel sorry for him now that he's been captured. Obviously, she has no idea what he's capable of. As usual, it's up to me to keep her safe. "Watch it, buster!" I bark at the prisoner. "Or you'll be sorry!"

Hattie pulls me back. "FEN-way!"

The Evil Bunny glowers at me, his nose twitching with wickedness. And—*thump!* His hind leg smacks the bottom of the cage.

Yikes! Could he attack from in there? I quiver with courage, my ears and tail drooping. "C-c-cut it out, y-y-you monster!" I snarl. "Or I'll pounce! Or . . . something."

"Shhhhh," Hattie murmurs, patting my neck.

It's nice to know she approves of my efforts.

Fetch Man and Food Lady give Hattie a look I know all too well. It's the same look they give whenever she feeds me from the table.

Hattie ignores their eyes. She sets me down and ushers me away from the cage. She turns to the tall humans and gestures at the Evil Bunny, like maybe they forgot he was there. She rattles the cage door, even though it's latched shut and not opening. She seems rather happy about it. That makes two of us.

Food Lady sighs. "Wah-chim," she says, then heads into the Eating Place.

The Evil Bunny keeps on growling. He's probably preparing to make his move.

I give him a sneer. But I take a few steps back. He may be in a cage, but he's obviously got sinister intentions. A dog can never be too careful.

Fetch Man puts an arm around Hattie. His chattering

voice sounds calm and soothing. And slightly bossy. He almost seems like he's trying to protect her—as if there weren't already a professional on the job.

While Hattie's distracted by Fetch Man, I keep my gaze fully on the Evil Bunny. He'd better not try anything while I'm around. Luckily, he's still cowering in the corner.

Soon sizzling noises waft in from the Eating Place. Delectable aromas of spicy chicken, yummy cheese, and creamy sour cream waft in, too. Yippee! Tacos! I love tacos! My tummy grumbles. My tail thumps. My tongue drips with anticipation.

As we charge into the Eating Place, Hattie glances back anxiously at the Evil Bunny. Is she worried he might escape?

I glance back, too. He doesn't seem to be going anywhere. But even if he did manage to break out, my expert skills would track him down in a flash. And then there'd be trouble! I shiver at the thought.

We gather around the table as Food Lady serves crispy tortillas, savory chicken, and melt-y cheese. I perch next to Hattie's seat, my mouth watering, and wait for tasty bits to fall.

As the humans get busy munching and chatting, suspicious sounds drift in from the Lounging Place. My ears perk in alarm, but Hattie goes on chomping her taco, apparently unconcerned. I creep into the hallway, peering at the wire cage.

Aha! The Evil Bunny's using the humans' taco diversion as an opportunity to prowl through the hay. He's clearly up to something. I knew he couldn't be trusted.

"Fenway, come!" Hattie calls.

I tear back into the Eating Place to the exciting sound of food rattling into my dish. YUM! I dive into the tasty deliciousness, my ears up just in case. With the Evil Bunny so close to my short human, I must be vigilant.

After supper, while Food Lady and Fetch Man clank pans and plates, Hattie opens the tall humming box with cold food inside. Frosty air bursts out.

I'm at her side in a flash. Whoopee! Is ice cream coming? I love ice cream!

But instead of yummy ice cream or vanilla pudding, she grabs an armful of icky carrots, celery, and lettuce. She sets them on the counter.

I cock my head, watching, as she studies that folded page from her pocket. She snaps and tears the icky vegetables and places them on a paper plate.

I follow her into the Lounging Place and straight over to the cage. Hattie makes "kitchy-koo" noises.

She wiggles a carrot through the bars. That's my girl! Torturing the prisoner with a yucky vegetable!

Hattie tosses the carrot onto the hay. Lettuce leaves and celery stalks, too. The Evil Bunny takes the bait and begins nibbling. "Thum-per, Thum-per," Hattie sings.

Thum-per? Thumper? Why does she keep saying that? What could it mean?

Hattie pokes a finger into the cage and strokes his nasty fur some more. The way she's treating him is almost . . . loving.

But it couldn't be, unless he's fooled her somehow. I jump up and claw the cage. "I'm on to you, prisoner!" I bark, baring my teeth. "I know you're up to no good."

"FEN-way!" Hattie swoops me into her arms. I'm about to tell her that I was only trying to help when through the window I spy a distraction. Across the street, Whisker Face and Round Lady are rushing out their front door. Whisker Face is holding a bulky bag in one hand and guiding Round Lady to the driveway with the other. Her arm is draped over her round belly, her face focused on the car. They seem harried. And hurried.

Hattie gasps with excitement. "Look! Look!" she calls.

Fetch Man and Food Lady get to the window in time

to see the car backing onto the street and zooming away. The humans practically bounce with glee. Why are they happy our neighbors are fleeing? The Evil Bunny isn't in their house anymore. Or are they running from the rest of the gang?

I quake at the thought.

As the sky grows dark, I run to every window I can reach. The gang is out there. I have to be ready.

When it's bedtime, Hattie goes to carry the cage upstairs. But Fetch Man and Food Lady boss her into the Eating Place instead.

Hattie begs and begs, but they shake their heads. They point at the table, which is curiously draped with old towels.

Her shoulders slumped, Hattie sets the cage on the table. "Thum-per, Thum-per," she sings sweetly, her face smooshing into the bars. If this is supposed to be tormenting him, she's doing a pretty bad job of it.

After a long, sad look at Fetch Man and Food Lady, Hattie trudges to the stairs. I leap on her legs. She smells as disappointed as I feel.

"How can we guard the prisoner if we're up there and he's down here?" I bark.

She must not have an answer, because she keeps going up the stairs. After a stop in the Bathtub Room, we climb into bed. Hattie kisses my front paws. She brushes my fur and sings, "Best buddies, best buddies." She smells strongly of mint.

I sigh into each luxurious stroke. My eyes start to close but pop open again with a terrifying thought. Now that we've captured one Evil Bunny, what will happen when the gang finds out?

Chapter 7

The next morning, Hattie jumps into her clothes. She's halfway through the door, then whips back to her dresser.

After slipping on the sparkly bracelet, she practically flies down the stairs and into the Eating Place. And I'm pretty sure it's not because she's hungry.

I go to help check on the prisoner, but she shoos me out the back door and slides it shut. Does she think she can handle that monster on her own?

I'm about to whine for her attention, but then something makes my hackles flare up. The Dog Park reeks of trouble. Is the Evil Bunny Gang invading already?

A nasty swish catches my eye. Whew! I'm strangely relieved that it's only a squirrel. I'm after him like a shot.

"I've warned you all before," I bark, racing through the grass. "No squirrels allowed!"

He sits up tall, his unblinking eyes scowling at me. He's got a lot of nerve.

I'm ready to snap when he flicks his tail in defiance. He scurries to the top of the fence and throws himself over the side.

"Coward!" I bark, leaping up and clawing the slats. When I'm sure he's really gone, I go after the real target—the Evil Bunny Gang.

I sniff around the bushes. I have to remain on guard. As long as we hold the prisoner, they're likely to retaliate. At any time!

Snap!

Whoa. Was that a twig breaking behind the giant tree? I freeze mid-sniff, listening. And trembling.

I remind myself that I'm a professional. If there's even the slightest sign of evil or danger, it's my job to find it. Those villains don't stand a chance against me. I sniff my way around the giant tree and along the back fence. The traces of bunny are scant and faint. Clearly, they're still gone. For the time being.

Click! The Friend Gate swings open. Angel's face is tilted up at the falling white ball. *Thwap!* She snags it in her fat glove. She runs up to the porch and leans her face against the screen door. "Hattie?" she calls.

Goldie and Patches hurry over, tails swinging.

"Ladies!" I cry. They huddle around me for the daily greetings.

I drop down on my front legs. A gleam in her eye, Patches leaps up, and we tumble in the grass.

"So, Fenway," Goldie says. "Found any 'Evil Bunnies' lately?"

I flip over, my fur standing on end. "Why do you ask?"

Goldie gazes at me sideways. "Um, because you've been obsessed with them."

"And it's a good thing, too," I say. "The Dog Park is bunny-free. For now."

Patches licks my muzzle. "I still think you're over-reacting, but your heart's in the right place," she says kindly.

"Overreacting? Listen to this!" I lower my voice in case the gang might overhear. "There's one inside our house. In a cage!"

"You're not serious," Goldie says with a grimace.

Patches's eyes widen. "A cage, you say?"

"My Hattie captured him all by herself," I tell them. "And he's a totally obnoxious prisoner, too. He made a terrible racket. Probably trying to alert the rest of them. Or escape."

Goldie and Patches share a disbelieving glance.

Patches turns back to me, her face pained. "Fenway, are you sure . . . ?"

"Look, ladies, I don't want to brag," I say. "But I have a certain amount of expertise when it comes to pests. My squirrel-chasing skills are legendary."

"That's for sure," Goldie cuts in.

"The bunnies clearly operate the same as squirrels. In evil gangs. Once word gets out that we have one of them . . . if the news hasn't gotten out already"— I shoot a quick peek at the back fence before going on—"the rest of the gang will surely try to chase us away and rescue him. They've already scared off the neighbors!"

"You sound awfully certain about that," Patches says.

"I saw it with my own eyes!" My tail rises with the realization. "I'll bet the one Hattie captured is their leader!"

Patches tilts her head in disbelief.

"It's the only thing that makes sense," I say. "Hattie calls him a strange word—*Thumper*. That must mean *Leader of the Evil Bunny Gang.*"

"Or it could be his name," Goldie says with a sneer.

I glare at them. "You ladies obviously don't know bunnies. I have to be ready." I thrust out my chest. "I have to make sure the gang doesn't strike."

"Um, Fenway, about the *prisoner* . . ." Goldie gruffs.

"Do you think he might actually be a new member of the family?"

"No way!" I cock my head. "He's an Evil Bunny! How could he be part of our family?"

Goldie and Patches share another glance. Then Patches turns to me. "It happens," she says in her loveliest, kindest voice. "Humans bring home new animals. The others learn to accept it."

I shudder. "We're talking about an Evil Bunny!" I cry. "Hattie would never do that."

Patches gazes at me, her expression wise and gentle. "What would you do if she did?"

"That's impossible!" I say, trying to make myself taller. "Hattie cares for me. I'm all she needs."

Goldie gazes at Patches. "That's what I used to say." She wanders off and sprawls out in the grass with a sigh.

"What's gotten into her?" I ask Patches.

"That's a story for another time," she says. She plucks a stick, clearly expecting me to chase her around the Dog Park.

How can I play at a time like this? That Evil Bunny Gang might be plotting their invasion. They could be tunneling into the Dog Park at any moment. I have way too much work to do.

I trot along the back fence where I last smelled the

Evil Bunny Gang. I paw the dirt, digging for clues. If those bunnies are planning an attack, I'll be ready.

Goldie and Patches are not professionals. They don't understand evil creatures the way I do. Thumper is obviously a prisoner. Why else would he be trapped in a cage?

I sprint over to the wire fence that surrounds the vegetable patch. It smells a lot like the lettuce Hattie fed the prisoner last night. The Evil Bunnies caused the trouble with the plants in this very spot. That was probably just the beginning.

I begin to dig alongside the vegetable patch, sniffing like crazy. If those criminals have returned, I'll be the first to know.

F-f-f-f-t! The sliding door opens. Hattie appears on the porch. She pulls on her cap and grabs her fat leathery glove. Except for Angel's jacket and Hattie's bare arms, the two short humans are dressed exactly alike.

Or actually there's one other exception.

Hattie's stuffing her hand in the glove when Angel points at her sparkly wrist. "What's that?" she says, her nose scrunched up.

Flinching, Hattie slips off the bracelet and shoves it in her pocket. "Nothing," she mutters, then races off to the other side of the Dog Park.

Angel tosses the white ball. *Thwap!* It lands in Hattie's glove.

Hattie clutches the ball like a prize. She winds up and throws it back to Angel. "Woot!" she cries when Angel snags it. "Fenway, park!" She twirls and dances around.

Hooray! Hooray! Finally, the park! I start to romp over, my tail going nuts. But the short humans aren't going anywhere. They just keep playing ball. Probably for the best. I have way too much to do!

I trot to the vegetable patch. I have some bunnies to stop.

Apparently, the ladies have given up trying to talk me out of it. Goldie's still sighing in the corner while Patches is busy scratching herself. The short humans are whooping and hollering and having fun. I run the length of the side fence, sniffing the dirt. If those villains are even thinking of tunneling in again, I'll detect them.

Thwap! Hattie snags the ball, twirling around. She hurls the ball back at Angel.

Aha! My nose stops at a very interesting spot along the back fence, near the used-to-be hole. My fur bristles. The bunny stench is unmistakable. Good thing I'm on the job!

I claw the ground, digging furiously. The Evil Bunny Gang is probably right on the other side of the fence! I can hardly wait to see their cowardly bunny faces when a fierce Jack Russell Terrier shows up! I dig and dig, the hole getting wider and deeper . . .

Right then, the screen door slides open. "Stop! FEN-way! Stop!" Food Lady yells. She races across the porch and into the Dog Park. "Hattie!" she cries, waving her arms.

"What the—?" Hattie shouts. Her leathery glove falls to the ground as she rushes over.

In a flash, Food Lady's at my side, grabbing my collar and pulling me away from the hole. I twist and squirm, for all the good it does. "Wah-chim?" she says to Hattie, sighing in frustration.

Hattie glares at me. "FEN-way," she growls.

What's she mad at me for? I'd be finishing the job right now if Food Lady hadn't interfered.

Food Lady and Hattie take turns talking. They are both upset. Angel must realize Hattie's done playing because she rounds up Goldie and Patches and they head through the Friend Gate.

Click! Playtime is over.

Chapter 8

Food Lady hands me over to Hattie as if
that's somehow helping the situation. My humans are
obviously unaware of the very real threat. Maybe they
think now that the gang leader's been captured, we can
sit back and relax. Or leave the Dog Park unguarded.

Because that's what they're doing. "This is not right,"
I bark, wiggling furiously as we head into the house. "I
can't prevent the Evil Bunny Gang from attacking if I'm
stuck inside!"

Hattie slides the door shut behind us and breezes
into the Eating Place. Food Lady points at my dirty
paws and shoos us into the hallway.

"On it," Hattie says, making a guilty face. She whisks
me upstairs and into . . . the Bathtub Room? I start kicking. "Hey, what'd I do to deserve this?" I bark.

I protest until it's clear she's going for a big fluffy towel and not putting me in the dreaded bathtub. Hattie rubs me all over until hardly any of the wonderful dirt is left.

I burrow into the cozy towel as Hattie rubs me some more. Oh yeah, that's the spot. I'm enjoying the massage so much, I almost forget about the danger we are facing.

When we get back to the Eating Place, Hattie lifts me up dramatically. "See?" she says as if Food Lady might be surprised that I'm relatively clean.

Food Lady gives a quick nod of approval, her eyes barely glancing up from a small flashing screen and her fingers splayed and dancing on the counter.

I squirm out of Hattie's grasp and spring onto the floor. Now that I'm inside, the Evil Bunny Gang is probably roaming freely in the Dog Park, preparing their assault at this very moment.

I race to the back door as I hear the clinky-clacky sounds of Hattie putting dishes away. While she's distracted, I press against the screen door, searching for clues.

But I haven't had a chance to find any when Hattie grabs me. "What?" I bark in protest as she sets me down in the Eating Place. Right next to the table. And the cage.

That Evil Bunny is scrounging in the hay. I can

smell his aggression all the way down here. He is clearly plotting against us.

Hattie leans over, smiling. "Thum per, Thum per," she coos.

Before Thumper has a chance to react, I assume attack posture. "Don't even think of trying anything!" I bark.

"Fenway!" Hattie cries, her voice surprised. Did she forget I was right next to her?

Thumper looks up, then hops to the front of the cage. His piercing eyes glare down at me. He lifts his chubby hind leg . . . *thump!*

I snarl. "Why, of all the obnoxious—"

Thump! Thump! Thump!

"Fenway, shhh," Hattie says in a calming voice. She sneaks a sheepish glance over at Food Lady. She whisks me up and brings me right to the cage. Does she think I need help?

"I was doing just fine way down there on the floor," I bark, trying to hide a slight shiver.

"Awww," Hattie coos. She clutches me tight, like we're all having a happy time together and there's no trouble going on. She brings me closer to the Evil Bunny, babbling sweetly. "Thum-per, Thum-per," she sings in my ear. She sounds so encouraging. What's she trying to tell me?

There's no time to figure it out. I'm nose to nose with pure evil! I give the bunny my best snarl.

Hattie sticks her fingers into the cage. To my horror, Thumper wiggles his whiskers in a way that can only be described as menacing. Is he about to bite?

Luckily, I'm poised to strike. He'd better not try it!

As Hattie pets his floppy ears, the nasty fur ball starts making a low humming sound. Not clicking or clacking like before. He's purring!

I creep up Hattie's arm, growling. "Look, you monster!" I bark. "You're not fooling anybody with that cat impression. We're totally on to you!"

Food Lady turns away from the flashing screen. "Hattie!" she scolds. Does she suddenly realize the danger Hattie's in?

Hattie pulls her fingers out of the cage like they're on fire. She steps back, making a sorry face at Food Lady, who scrunches up her nose as if she just noticed how bad this imposter smells, too.

Food Lady points down the hall and goes over to the sink, where water begins whooshing into a pot.

I'm not sure what's going on, but Food Lady must be getting through to Hattie. She sets me down, then lifts up the cage and carries it out of the room.

I follow Hattie down the hall, my tail swishing with excitement. I can hardly wait to see where we're going.

Will we toss the Evil Bunny into the garbage? Dump him in the woods? He deserves much worse. We must get rid of him once and for all!

Hattie ducks into the little Washing Room. Yippee! I leap and twirl. We're going to flush him down the deep gurgling bowl! I knew Hattie'd have an awesome plan. I wish I'd thought of it!

Hattie puts the cage on the counter next to the sink. Very carefully, she opens the little door.

Wowee! I'm jumping on her legs, panting. I don't want to miss one single second of the action. That Evil Bunny is going to get exactly what's coming to him.

He must realize what's happening. As soon as Hattie reaches into the cage, he shies away from her hand. He huddles in the corner, glowering. And growling.

Like we'd be intimidated by the likes of him. I keep jumping on Hattie's legs. If that sinister fur ball thinks we're going to back down, he's even more deranged than I thought.

But instead of seizing him, Hattie gathers up the partially chewed carrots and shreds of lettuce.

Thumper gives her a beady-eyed glare of protest.

Unfazed, Hattie dumps soggy paper into the trash. Why isn't she getting the job done? Could she be having second thoughts about flushing him? Or is she simply prolonging his agony?

I can't stand not knowing. I run in circles, skidding on the mat and nearly crashing into a cabinet.

As Hattie drops clumps of wet hay in the garbage, Thumper continues his ridiculous growling. Hissing, too. He burrows into what's left of the paper.

I leap as high as I can. Even though there's no way I can reach the counter, I have to show him who's in charge. "Surrender, bunny!" I bark. "Accept your fate!"

"Shhh, Fenway," Hattie whispers, looking nervously at the door. Is she expecting the Evil Bunny Gang to show up?

Trembling, I creep to her side and peek down the hall. But I don't see any signs of them.

Hattie turns back and reaches into the cage again. Making a sweet face, she coos at that Evil Bunny. She grabs the empty bowl and splashes it in the sudsy sink. She does the same with the plastic bottle.

Thumper must realize she's distracted, because he hops up to the front of the cage and starts nibbling on the bars. His eyes glare at us, shiny and vicious, full of determination. He's trying to escape!

"You've had your last warning!" I bark. I spring into action, my jaws ready to snap. As I leap for the cabinet, I bump against a tall stand that immediately wobbles and teeters and . . .

Smash! Crash!

Suddenly, the tall stand is leaning against the wall. Spools of soft paper are unrolling across the floor. Along with oozing lotions and foamy liquids. Which smell terrible, like flowers. And soap!

"*Eeeeeeeeee!*" the prisoner squeals.

Hattie's hands fly up to her face, her eyes wide in horror.

I know that look. She's going to be mad. I scoot away from the mess.

But Hattie doesn't yell. She does something much more disturbing. She reaches into the cage. "Thumper," she soothes, stroking his quivering fur.

I back into the corner, repulsed. Hattie is comforting this nasty creature. Why? From what?

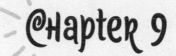

Chapter 9

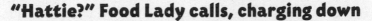

"Hattie?" Food Lady calls, charging down the hall. Her voice is full of concern.

"Eep," Hattie murmurs, smelling worried. Is she upset about Food Lady? The mess on the floor? Thumper? It's impossible to know.

Hattie turns toward the door. Her mouth opens to say something when—

Ding-dong! Ding-dong!

My hackles shoot up. Intruders!

Food Lady pokes her head into the Washing Room, her eyebrows jumping in alarm. Hattie rushes to the front door. I race behind her.

"Zahra," Hattie says, her chest pounding.

Zahra steps into the Lounging Place, the rattly box under her arm. Yippee! Is Zahra here to play?

"Awww, Fenway," Zahra says. She bends down and pets me.

Food Lady appears and shoots a questioning look at Hattie.

Hattie deflates. She looks at Zahra, her face sad. "Too-bizz-ee," she says.

Zahra's shoulders sink. Her face looks just as glum as Hattie's. She turns and goes away.

Food Lady sighs. She speaks to Hattie, sounding exasperated.

Hattie glances away nervously. She chatters and chatters and chatters.

Food Lady's eyes narrow. She looks skeptical. She takes in a breath, like she's about to speak again, when suddenly the Eating Place goes *Beep! Beep! Beep!* After wagging a finger, Food Lady rushes off toward the scent of boiling potatoes.

"Let's go," I bark, racing back down the hallway. "We have an Evil Bunny to deal with!"

Hattie groans and chases me down the hall. Finally, we can get back to work!

But when we get to the Washing Room, Hattie dashes in and shuts the door. Right on my snout!

I scratch the door frame. "Hey, what about me?" I bark.

The door opens a crack. Hattie's head pops out, her finger to her lips. "Shhh!"

The door shuts again.

I sink down and cock my head. From under the door, I hear sounds of water whooshing and stopping, whooshing and stopping. Hattie must be disposing of the Evil Bunny on her own. It doesn't sound like a struggle . . . yet. Though with bunnies, anything could happen!

Hattie needs my help. She could be in danger at this very moment! I have to get to her! I pace back and forth, desperate for an idea.

I'm nearly exhausted from pacing, without any ideas at all, when it occurs to me that I haven't heard one single bunny noise. Could he already be gone? Down the drain? Out the window? There are millions of ways she could've gotten rid of him. I start panting with excitement.

I leap to my feet and spin in circles. Whoopee! That must be it! It's the Best News Ever!

And then, mid-celebration, a terrible thought nips at me. I stop short.

I didn't hear any loud swishing or gurgling. Or the *pfffft!* of the window opening. Is he really gone?

I must find out. "Hattie! Hattie!" I bark. "Hurry out! I can't stand the suspense." I claw and scratch furiously against the door. "Tell me what happened!"

I barely jump out of the way as the door flies open and Hattie steps out. She's carrying that big cage.

Is it empty?

I leap on her legs for a better sniff. I smell soap. And Evil Bunny.

I gaze up at the cage. Hateful eyes glare back at me. I shiver.

Hattie pushes her face into the bars. "Thum-per, Thum-per," she sings. Her voice is happy and cooing and not the least bit concerned that the mission failed.

At lunch, Hattie scarfs down a peanut butter and jelly sandwich, even though Food Lady's at the counter with what smells like a delicious, creamy potato salad. With hard-boiled eggs on top. She hides the huge bowl in the tall humming box like she doesn't want us to eat it.

Afterward, Food Lady hands Hattie a broom and bosses us out onto the porch. No matter how much I prance and coax, Hattie's in no mood to play. Her face weary, she glances around at the tangled jump rope, the muddy sneakers, the sweatshirt, and a whole bunch of other stuff. She sighs, like she has a big job to do.

Of course, I have a big job of my own.

I gallop into the grass and get busy sniffing around the back fence. With their leader trapped in the house, the Evil Bunny Gang is bound to break in and try to spring him. But they'll have to get past me first. I'll be all over those trespassing bunnies. Like fur!

I'm casing the perimeter of the Dog Park, hunting for signs of them, when I find a suspicious patch of dirt. It's behind the giant tree along the back fence where that tunnel was. At first the soft soil smells slightly Hattie-ish, but as I dig deeper, I get a stronger whiff of bunny.

"FEN-way!" Hattie yells, sprinting through the grass. Her eyes are wide with alarm.

"I'm on it, Hattie!" I quickly burrow into the hole. There's no time to waste!

Hattie grabs me by the collar and yanks me out. "No!" she shouts. She gazes up at the house, smelling anxious.

"Don't worry," I bark, straining to get back to work. "I'll take care of them this time."

Apparently, my furious kicking and wriggling don't reassure her one bit. She finds a big rock, then squats next to the hole and shoves it in. "Leave it!" she demands. Her voice is mad.

I slink away, my head hanging, my tail sagging. It's so unfair! I'm just trying to help.

Hattie shakes an angry finger, then trudges back to the mess on the porch. As soon as her back is turned, I sneak behind a bush. Hattie might think she can handle the Evil Bunny on her own, but she must not realize that we're up against a whole gang.

I'm sniffing for another promising spot to dig when the Friend Gate swings open. Angel barrels through, followed by Goldie and Patches! I trot over to meet them.

After we finish the circle-sniff dance, Patches stands back. "What's the problem, Fenway?" she says, her face concerned.

"Let me guess," Goldie says, glancing back at Hattie. "More bunny trouble?"

My ears sag. "You could say that."

"Come on!" Angel shouts, and we turn. She gestures up at Hattie's little house in the giant tree, a gleam in her eye. She runs over to the trunk and waves for Hattie to follow.

Angel grabs on to the rungs that lead to the way-up-high branches. She keeps shouting to Hattie, "Come on!" as she climbs.

But Hattie stays put on the porch, watching with sad eyes. Her shoulders are slumped. Her face is full of longing.

Patches turns to Goldie. "I suppose that's the

bunny's fault, too?" she says in a voice that does not sound lovely at all.

Goldie humphs. "I wouldn't be surprised. Newcomers usually mess things up."

"Or struggle to fit in," Patches says, bordering on grouchy.

Whoa. The ladies disagree sometimes—or maybe even most of the time—but they're family. I can't shake the feeling that something else is going on.

"Hattie!" Angel's voice calls from the leafy branches. "Come on!"

Hattie appears to think for a second. She glances nervously at the window. Then she rushes around the porch, gathering all the stuff and piling it in the corner. She sweeps the broom once or twice, then tosses it aside. After another quick glance over her shoulder, she races to the giant tree and starts climbing.

"So, Fenway," Goldie says, sinking casually into the grass. "What's going on with the bunny?"

"He's still trapped in the cage, but I have to be on guard against the others." I sneak a look at the back fence. "I've sniffed and sniffed. I've dug around in every hole. The Evil Bunny Gang won't catch me by surprise."

"Digging holes?" Patches interrupts, her lovely voice returning, full of concern. "Do you really think that's a good idea? You could get scolded. Or worse!"

"Listen, Fenway," Goldie says. "You're facing a way bigger threat than bunnies tunneling under the fence."

My fur stiffens. "What could be worse than a Gang of Evil Bunnies?"

Goldie gapes at me for a second like I asked a dumb question. Or maybe she has to think about the answer. "Um, let me put it this way," she says. "Has your short human been treating you differently lately?"

"Differently? How do you mean?"

"You know," Goldie says. "Not playing with you, not appreciating you, and worst of all, paying attention to *him*?"

I cock my head, trying to remember. She didn't yell when that noisy mess happened in the Washing Room. That was different. But then the image of Hattie comforting the bunny floats into my head, and I shudder.

Goldie stares at me, a horrible look of self-satisfaction on her face.

"So what?" I say, not meeting her gaze. "He's our prisoner! Hattie has to pay attention to him. We can't let him escape!"

Patches nudges her way between us. "Think about it, Fenway. Is she guarding Thumper? Or taking care of him?"

I drop down for a quick scratch. And a think. Patches doesn't know what she's talking about. There's no way

Hattie would—*gulp*—care for that bunny. And what's the threat Goldie said was worse than a Gang of Evil Bunnies?

I'm listening to Hattie's giggles floating down from the leafy branches when I hear another sound. *F-f-f-f-t—bang!* And Hattie gasps.

CHapteR 10

Food Lady stands on the porch, her arms crossed. We all focus on her. "Hattie?" Food Lady calls in an angry tone.

Hattie climbs down the giant tree like it's a race. Angel's right behind her. "Sah-ree," Hattie says, her voice drooping with sadness. And hope.

Food Lady scowls at Hattie's things piled in the corner. She glances at the broom lying on the floor. She sucks in a breath, then says three words that I know: "No," "Fenway," and "park."

Hattie gulps. "No! Please-please-please!" she cries, her eyes getting glassy as she marches to the porch. She sounds desperate.

Food Lady shakes her head. Apparently, she doesn't

want to listen. She hands Hattie the broom and heads back inside.

Hattie holds the broom with one hand and wipes her eyes with the other. Between sniffles, she mumbles to Angel, "Sah-ree."

Angel looks as miserable as Hattie sounds. Angel heads toward the Friend Gate, motioning for the ladies to follow.

"See you later, Fenway," Patches says, trotting after Angel.

Goldie isn't far behind.

"Wait!" I say to Goldie. "You haven't told me what the threat is."

"Later," Goldie says under her breath.

I plop down in the grass and watch our friends disappear through the gate.

There's no question about it—Hattie is upset. Clearly, she needs a fun game of fetch. Or chase. But keeping her safe is a higher priority right now.

I charge up to the fence. Through the slats, I spot Goldie rolling around in the grass. Patches is at the other end of their Dog Park, chewing on a stick. Angel is nowhere to be seen. "Tell me, Goldie," I say.

She flips onto her side, her snout pointed at the fence. "Are you sure you really want to know?" she says.

I meet her gaze. "Of course."

"Okay." Goldie pushes herself upright and steps closer. "Prepare yourself, little guy. You're not gonna like it."

My bumpy collar itches, but I ignore it. "Spit it out, Goldie. What threat could be bigger than a Gang of Evil Bunnies?"

Goldie takes a hesitating breath. "The one in the cage."

"Thumper?!" My fur bristles. "I knew it! He's infiltrated the house as part of a diabolical plot, hasn't he? Those bunnies are pure evil! They—"

"No, Fenway," Goldie interrupts. "That's not it."

I pace wildly along the fence. "It all makes sense. Now that he's on the inside, he's in the perfect position to launch the attack. He's probably got a secret way of signaling to the gang. Thanks to you, I can figure it out and stop them before it's too late!"

"Whoa, Fenway," Goldie says. "Slow down. You've got it all wrong."

"Wrong?" I press my nose into the gap between the slats. "What are you talking about?"

"That bunny isn't in the house to attack," she says. "Your short human wants him there."

"Obviously," I say. "Hattie's keeping him prisoner."

Goldie cocks her head. "Believe me, Fenway. He's not a prisoner."

"Well, if he's not a prisoner, why would Hattie capture him and bring him home?"

Goldie sneaks a look over at Patches, who's still chewing on her stick. "Because he's little and cute and cuddly. She wants to pet him and play with him and snuggle him."

My hackles shoot up. "That's impossible! She does those things with me. She loves only me. She doesn't want anybody else, especially not an Evil Bunny!"

"Fenway, I don't blame you for being in denial." Goldie sighs. "It's hard to accept that your short human could love somebody else."

"Hattie would never do that. She has me! She doesn't need him or anyone!"

Goldie's quiet for a moment, then gazes into the distance like she's remembering something. "You think that now," she mutters.

"I'll think that forever," I say with a growl. I turn away and sink down in the grass. Goldie doesn't know anything. Hattie could never care about a—a—a bunny.

Later, Food Lady shoos Hattie upstairs with a stack of clean-smelling clothes. I follow along. She still looks glum, but it's my job to change that. "I've got a great idea, Hattie," I bark, racing to her room. "Let's play tug-of-war!"

"Fenway!" Hattie rushes after me. Yippee! I knew she'd be up for it.

I dash through the door, my tail swishing with glee. I zip over a sneaker, hop around a tower of books, and chomp down on one end of a damp towel. Ha! I tear across the room, the towel whipping along behind me. It smacks against the dresser, the chair, the desk.

Hattie can hardly control her excitement. She grabs the other end of the towel as it snakes through a storm of flying clothes, over a stack of scattering books, and behind the tipping trash can. She pulls with all her might. "Fenway!" she growls.

I go to leap onto the bed but—*oof!*—I fall back to the floor; the towel drops out of my mouth.

"Ha!" Hattie cries, her eyes glowing in triumph. She grabs the towel before I can recover.

"Hey, I let you win," I bark. And judging by how satisfied Hattie looks, this was exactly the right strategy.

But Hattie's victory is short-lived. She gazes at the floor, sighing at the mess. Her face is full of frustration.

Clearly, I have more work to do. I spring onto the bed. "I have another great idea, Hattie," I bark. "Let's snuggle."

Apparently, she's got other things on her mind. With a loud huff, she grabs some clothes off the floor and starts refolding them. Right then, a gleeful *Woot!* drifts in through the window screen. My ears perk.

I climb onto the ledge to check it out. Hattie squeezes in beside me. Down below, our Dog Park is empty. But the Dog Park next door is not.

Patches is snoozing near the back fence. Goldie is curled up on the porch. Both ladies look bored and unhappy, not romping or tumbling the way they usually do.

And that isn't the only difference.

Angel, wearing her cap and glove, is gently tossing a ball . . . not with Hattie but—*Zahra*? I almost didn't recognize her in that cap. But I'd know her white dress and sparkly bracelets anywhere.

Zahra's silky black hair hangs in a long tail behind her head. She slips into a jacket—Angel's jacket!—and wields a fat glove, just like Angel's. She moves awkwardly toward the ball and catches it. To her apparent surprise.

"Woot!" Angel cries, pumping her fist.

As I crane my neck for a better view, Hattie draws in a breath.

Zahra holds her glove in the air. She spins around, her white dress poofing out under Angel's jacket like an umbrella.

Hattie goes to call out to them but abruptly changes her mind when Angel reaches into her pocket. Angel pulls out two strips and offers them to Zahra like treats.

Hattie gasps. Her hands clamp onto her cheeks.

"*My*-tick-it," she murmurs. "Fenway, park." She smells horrified. And miserable.

It makes no sense. Taking me to the park is fun. Why isn't Hattie happy?

Well, it's my job to fix that. I chomp the used-to-be bear and spring off the bed. Keep-away is Hattie's favorite game.

I romp into the middle of the room, scamper through the clean clothes, and leap over book after book after book. I waggle the used-to-be bear. She won't be able to resist!

But somehow she does. Hattie paces back and forth, her shoulders heaving, her nose sniffling.

I have to step up my efforts! I jump onto an open book, and *r-r-rip!* A couple of pages tear.

"Fenway!" Hattie scolds, her cheeks wet and puffy.

She's clearly upset, but I can't give up now.

Before I can make another move, she yells, "Stop it, Fenway!" She flies from the room, shutting the door behind her.

"Hattie, you forgot me!" I bark.

But she doesn't answer. She doesn't come.

I'm pawing the door to get her attention when I notice it's not latched. It takes a lot of hard work, but I manage to nose it open.

I race downstairs, searching for her. But the entryway,

the Lounging Place, and the hallway are all empty.

And when I burst into the Eating Place, I freeze in my tracks.

Hattie is standing over the cage. But the Evil Bunny isn't inside.

He's snuggled under her chin. "Thumper, Thumper," she whispers, sobbing. She rocks him from side to side, nuzzling her nose into his fur. Cuddling him.

My heart roars in pain.

CHapter 11

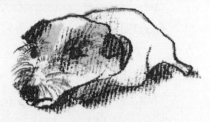

I collapse onto the floor. Goldie was right!
I knew that bunny was trouble! But I never thought he'd
come between me and my beloved short human. It's the
Worst News Ever.

He is nestled in Hattie's arms. He's stolen my job
of making Hattie happy. Or so he thinks. It's beyond
revolting. Does he actually expect me to roll over and
play dead?

Not on his Evil Bunny life! I jump up, hackles raised. I
leap on Hattie's legs. "This short human is mine!" I bark.
"And I'll never let you have her. Not without a fight!"

"FEN-way!" Hattie yells, pushing me away. "No!
No! No!" She shakes a scolding finger at me while

that villain snuggles in closer, his nose twitching in victory.

My ears sag. She's taking his side. My heart rips out all over again.

Right then, the car *vrooms* up the driveway. Hattie's eyebrows arch. She shoves the Evil Bunny back inside the cage mere moments before Fetch Man's voice calls from the garage. Hattie rushes to the back door.

"Fenway, come," she orders.

Yippee! We're going outside. Without him. Take that, Evil Bunny! She's loving me again. He may have burrowed his way into Hattie's heart, but no bunny can compete with the fun of a frolicking dog. "Enjoy that lonely cage while we go play!" I taunt.

I romp after Hattie into the Dog Park and over to the side gate. Fetch Man is pushing a shiny metal box with wheels on the bottom. Its front has knobs like the stove, and doors like the cabinets. My tail goes wild with curiosity! So does my nose!

Fetch Man's face is beaming with pride as he wheels the box through the grass. It looks like the barbecue that Whisker Face has across the street. Except its scent is new and boring and not wonderful like smoky hot dogs. Or barbecued chicken. Sadly, all I smell is metal.

Hattie shuts the gate. She runs to Fetch Man as he parks the barbecue. He lifts up the lid, revealing an empty grill. He pats Hattie on the back, his eyes glowing with excitement, even though there isn't any delicious food inside. Hattie forces a smile.

F-f-f-f-t! The door slides open. Food Lady steps out, one arm wrapped around a lumpy paper bag and the other carrying a big plastic bowl. She eyes the grill happily, like it was exactly what she was hoping to see.

Fetch Man chatters eagerly while Food Lady studies the shiny barbecue from top to bottom. They're both very excited. Don't they realize there's no tasty meat sizzling on it?

Food Lady passes the bag and bowl to Hattie, then disappears into the house. As Fetch Man heads back to the side gate, Hattie plops onto the porch steps and reaches into the crinkly bag.

Wowee! What if crunchy, munchy treats are inside? I rush over to investigate, my nose sniffing like crazy. I paw the paper till the bag tips and topples over, leafy logs rolling out. They smell grassy like husks and sweet like corn.

I've barely plunged in when Hattie grabs my collar and yanks me out. "FEN-way, no!" she scolds.

"Bad news, Hattie," I bark. "There's nothing in here except ears of corn."

Which apparently is not the only bad news. Hattie shakes her finger at me, her forehead scrunched. She sneaks a nervous glance at the side gate where Fetch Man disappeared.

I trot out into the grass and drop onto my forepaws. "Here's a great idea, Hattie!" I bark, my tail swishing. "Let's play chase!"

But Hattie isn't paying attention. She's focused on that bag of corn.

The side gate clicks open again, and Fetch Man returns, his arms cradling a chubby metal tank. He shoves it under the barbecue and hooks it up to a rubber hose.

"Come on, Hattie!" I gallop back to her and paw her knees. "You know you want to!"

After a quick glance at Fetch Man, Hattie gives me a stern look. "Shhh," she murmurs, pointing a corncob at me.

Talk about irresistible! I love tug-of-war! I chomp one end and dig my hind paws into the ground.

"FEN-way!" Hattie shrieks, her eyes darting from a disapproving Fetch Man, then back to me. "Drop it!"

I unclench my jaw, my heart crushing again. Hattie doesn't want to play with me.

Because she loves that Evil Bunny.

He probably doesn't even care about her. I'll bet he's only in it for the carrots.

I have to battle him. I have to win. There's nothing

I won't do to defeat my nemesis. But that's next to impossible when he's inside and I'm not.

I'm about to curl up and lick my wounds when my
nose gets wind of a familiar and horrifying bunny
stench. Is it drifting in from the Dog Park next door?
Hey, the Friend Gate is not closed all the way.

What if the Evil Bunny Gang noticed the open gate,
too? They could be on the other side of the fence at this
very moment. My tail shoots up.

I stick my snout through the crack. *Sniff . . . sniff . . .*
so many scents . . . the gang could definitely be in there.
I knew they'd be back! Have they come to free their
leader?

Free their leader? Ha! That's it! All this time, I've
been trying to prevent a bunny invasion. But it could
be exactly what I've been looking for—the gang can
do my dirty work! They'll help the Evil Bunny escape.
He'll be gone, and I'll have Hattie all to myself again.
Whoopee! It's the Best Idea Ever!

I glance back at the porch. Fetch Man's on his knees
fiddling with the chubby tank under the grill. Hattie's
telling him something in a sad voice. "My-tick-it," she
says as she brutally tears silky hairs off the corn. She
and Fetch Man are clearly distracted. Which can only
mean one thing—opportunity.

It's hard work, but I manage to nose my way through

the Friend Gate. Sniffing feverishly, I zig and zag across the ladies' Dog Park. That horrible scent is all over the place. Those Evil Bunnies are here somewhere. And when I find them, I'm going to lead them right to the prisoner!

I also detect strong odors of Goldie, Patches, Angel, and even me and Hattie. I pick up slight whiffs of Tool Man, Muffin Lady, and the occasional squirrel, too. And something else—recent scents of Angel's ball and another short human . . . Zahra.

I pause for a moment and sniff the air. Aha! I get back to work, rooting through the grass. That bunny stench is buried in the mixture of all the other smells, but it's here. And it's getting stronger.

Nose to the ground, I'm headed toward a cluster of vines near the house when suddenly I stop short. My hind leg is snagged on something, or rather *in* something. I squirm furiously, whipping my head back for a look.

Angel's jacket is dangling from the side of a lawn chair. With my paw caught in the pocket.

Talk about an obstacle. But no jacket can keep me from finding the Evil Bunny Gang! I pull. I tug. I must get loose!

I keep on yanking, but it's no use. All that happens is the jacket's arm swings and slaps me in the face. "Cut it out!" I bark.

Creeeeaaaaak! The Friend Gate swings open. Somebody's coming!

There's no time to lose. I bare my razor-sharp teeth. *Chomp!* I pull and pull until—*r-r-r-rip!*

The jacket falls to the grass and I scamper out of it. Whew! I knew my hard work would pay off.

"Fenway!" Hattie's voice calls. She sounds frantic, yet hushed at the same time. Her footsteps come up behind me.

I'm so close! I can't let her distract me! With the scent leading the way, I zoom toward the porch and dive into the tangly vines. Somewhere in this sweet, leafy aroma is the smell of Evil Bunnies. I've practically found them!

I've never been closer! I just need more time to nose around these vines. And then Hattie's hands close around me and pull me out.

CHAPTER 12

"Hey!" I bark, squirming wildly. "I was in
the middle of an important job!"

Hattie steals a worried glance around the ladies' Dog
Park. Is she afraid the Evil Bunny Gang will hear us?

She examines the rip in Angel's jacket, her eyes huge.
"Oh no!" she mutters. She hastily hangs it back on the
lawn chair as I thrash in her arms. I must get loose. I
was so close to finding those bunnies!

Hattie clutches me to her chest. She smells angry.
What's up with that? If anyone should be angry, it's me!
I'm sure I would've found the gang if she hadn't stopped
me! "Put me down!" I bark.

"Shhh," she murmurs again. We sneak across the

grass and slip through the Friend Gate. Which Hattie shuts with a soft *click*.

"Hattie, you don't understand," I bark as she sets me down in our own Dog Park. I rush back to the Friend Gate, leaping and pushing frantically. But it doesn't budge. "It's more important than ever!"

"FEN-way," Hattie snaps, wagging an angry finger at me. "Stay!"

"But I have to do my job," I wail.

Hattie heads back to the porch like she doesn't even hear me. She meets Fetch Man's concerned gaze, then immediately hangs her head. "Sah-ree," she mutters at him.

I slump in the grass and swipe at an annoying fly. It's obvious that Goldie was right. Hattie's stopped appreciating me. All because of *him*.

Hattie goes back to ripping long leaves and silky hair off the corn while Fetch Man plays with the barbecue. When the big bowl is overflowing with corncobs, Hattie carries it into the house.

Right then, my ears perk at promising sounds next door. The door slides open. Human footsteps pound. Dog tags jingle. And they're coming closer!

I race to the Friend Gate just as it clicks and swings open. Hooray! My friends are here! My tail swishes out of control.

Tool Man strides through the gate and over to Fetch Man, slapping his palm and patting him on the back. Muffin Lady, cradling a yummy-smelling basket, hurries to the porch. Food Lady greets her with a smile.

Angel appears wearing the familiar jacket, even though all the other humans are wearing bare arms. Hattie steps through the sliding doors carrying a stack of dishes. She eyes Angel warily, her gaze on the jacket.

Me and the ladies do the circle-sniff dance. Patches nuzzles my nose. "What's the matter, Fenway?" she asks in her lovely voice. "You smell distressed."

I shoot a glance at the humans. Fetch Man's proudly showing off the barbecue to a nodding Tool Man. Food Lady's leading Muffin Lady inside as Angel helps Hattie set dishes on the table. I turn back to the ladies. "You were right," I grumble to Goldie.

If she's surprised, she doesn't let on. "Wish I weren't," she says, sinking into the grass.

"Right about what?" Patches says. Could she not already know?

I glare at her. "The bunny, of course. Turns out he's evil, just as I suspected."

Patches cocks her head. "What has he done?"

"What has he *done*?" I jeer. "He's duped Hattie with his innocent little fur ball act. She's totally fallen for it. Next thing you know, she'll be playing chase with him and brushing his coat and cuddling with him at night!"

Goldie glowers. "What is it about short humans and new animals anyway? That's what I'd like to know."

I thrust out my chest. "But I won't stand for it! Hattie was mine first and I have rights!"

Patches looks concerned. "What do you plan to do?"

"Get rid of him!"

Patches's eyes widen in horror. "Fenway! You're not serious . . ."

Hiss! Pop! Our snouts turn in unison toward the sounds of sizzling meat. Our nostrils suck in the tantalizing aromas flaring up from the grill—smoky, delectable hamburgers! Savory-sweet hot dogs! My tongue drips uncontrollably. Talk about a distraction.

Goldie recovers first. "He's not serious about *what*, Patches? We're anxious to hear your dire warning."

My tail shoots up. "Warn all you want, but my mind's made up. I'm going to find the Evil Bunny Gang and lead them to Thumper. They'll take it from there."

"Hold on there," Patches says. "You're going to team up with a gang of bunnies?"

Goldie sneers at her. "I hate to agree, but have you thought this through, Fenway?"

I turn back with a sigh. "Well . . . maybe not. But I will. I have to. Too much is at stake!"

Goldie's ears flatten. "It's so sad," she says, her voice filled with pity. "You can't accept that she's moved on to somebody else."

I drop down and bury my nose in my paws.

"Poor guy." Goldie sinks down beside me. "Listen, fella. I know a thing or two about what you're going through."

I barely look up. "Yeah, right."

Goldie glances at Patches, who's watching intently. And keeping her mouth shut. Goldie nudges closer to me. "Look, Fenway. I was once in your paws. Back in the day, me and my precious Angel were inseparable. She couldn't get enough of me, playing and snuggling every day. We were everything to each other."

Goldie's eyes get sad. "Then one day, a new puppy showed up. Naturally, I shared my toys and bones and even my favorite cuddly blanket. I was as generous as a dog could be. But that puppy didn't appreciate my kindness one single bit."

"Um, there are two sides to every story," Patches butts in. "As I recall, I went out of my way to show you how grateful I was. And respectful."

"Ha!" Goldie shakes her head. "If by *respectful*, you mean ripping somebody else's belongings to shreds." She turns to me. "And did Little Patches get scolded even once? No! My precious Angel loved her and cuddled her no matter what she did."

I shudder. "Gosh, that's terrible."

Patches glowers at Goldie. "And you were never a puppy?"

"All I know is if I peed in the house or nibbled a sock, I'd get reprimanded," Goldie says. "But Little Patches could do no wrong. Angel couldn't resist those big puppy-dog eyes of hers."

"Unthinkable!" I say, remembering how mad Hattie got when that fuzzy bear's legs accidentally got chewed off.

"And I never once complained," Goldie continues as if Patches weren't standing right there listening. "I figured she was new and needed time to settle in. But all she ever did was yip and yap that I wasn't doing enough to make her feel welcome. Can you believe that?"

Patches's fur stiffens. "Hmm. Well, you were rather mean and bossy . . ."

"Humph!" Goldie looks away.

"Fenway, take it from me," Patches says. "If there's any lesson from our story, it's that things have a way of working themselves out. Be patient."

I tilt my head and think. Who could blame Goldie for being upset that a new animal came in and caused

trouble? And worse—that puppy stole her short human's love and affection! Goldie understands how
horrible that is, while Patches seems to think I should
make the best of it. It's pretty clear which one is looking
out for me.

"So what are you saying?" I ask Goldie.

Her eyes flash. "I'm saying if you don't do something,
that bunny is going to take over."

"Okay," I say. "But if teaming up with the Evil Bunny
Gang won't work, then what?"

"Well, I was thinking—" Goldie starts to say, but
Patches cuts her off.

"Wait a minute." Patches frowns. "Don't encourage
Fenway to do something he might regret."

"Stay out of this, Patches!" I growl, baring my teeth.

She backs off with an exaggerated yelp.

"FEN-way!" Hattie sprints toward us, her face
alarmed.

I snarl at Patches. "I'm not listening to you. You're
just trying to confuse me."

"Oh, Fenway. I'd never do that," she whimpers, shying
away.

Hattie pushes between us. "Stop it!" she scolds,
grabbing my bumpy collar.

Angel shoos Goldie, even though she didn't do

anything wrong. Then Angel hurries over to Patches and gives her a hug, eyeing me suspiciously.

"Hey, okay?" Fetch Man calls, looking up from the burgers.

"Yeah!" Hattie shouts back to him, smelling embarrassed. She whispers into my ear, "Bee-have . . ." Her shoulders slump. She sneaks a glance at Angel.

I keep my eyes on Patches. It's obvious whose side she's on. And it's not mine.

Food Lady emerges from the sliding doors carrying a steaming platter of corn. Muffin Lady's right behind her with a bowl that's piled high with something lumpy and white. Potato salad?

Food Lady calls everybody to the porch. Hattie and Angel exchange hesitant looks. Shrugging out of Angel's embrace, Patches wanders over to the vegetable patch and sulks next to the wire fence.

Hattie gazes into my eyes, her face stern. "Bee-have," she murmurs again before finally letting go of my collar.

Angel's halfway to the porch when Tool Man taps her on the shoulder. He spins her around, his hand petting a tear on her jacket.

Hattie freezes, her whole body reeking of fear.

Angel twists. She pulls the jacket off. "Oh no!" she cries, examining the rip.

Muffin Lady joins Tool Man at Angel's side. Their faces are full of concern. "How?" Muffin Lady asks.

Angel's eyes well up. "Zahra!" she cries.

Hattie opens her mouth like she's going to say something. But instead, she sucks in a shaky breath, then closes her lips. She smells scared and relieved at the same time.

Chapter 13

Barbecues are supposed to be exciting.
And delicious. But this one is the exact opposite.

Instead of happily munching her hot dog, a glum Hattie pushes her supper around on her plate. I slink over to lick up the ketchup-y droppings, but she shoos me away.

Patches apparently decides it's a perfect time for a nap. Goldie doesn't even bother perching next to Angel, who barely notices her hamburger. All she wants to look at is the tear in the back of that jacket.

The tall humans are the only ones chattering and chomping on creamy potato salad and ears of buttery corn. They must not realize everything's wrong.

When the sky gets dark and the crickets start

chirping, not even a vanilla cupcake or a gooey roasted marshmallow can get the short humans to smile. Goldie leaves me with words of sympathy and encouragement before they head home.

My family streams into the Eating Place, where I manage to plow through a bowl of yummy kibble even though the prisoner is acting more obnoxious than usual. He rustles through the hay and knocks over a dish—*clunk!* And if that's not horrible enough, his teeth start scraping against the cage—*scri-i-i-i-itch* . . . *scri-i-i-i-itch* . . . *scri-i-i-i-itch* . . .

Eeeee-yoooow! That sound is so annoyingly painful, every strand of fur on my back rises in protest.

While Food Lady's busy swishing a pan in the sink, Hattie goes to the cage. After a quick glance at Food Lady, Hattie leans over the Evil Bunny and sticks a finger through the bars. "Lay-ter," she whispers, gently patting his floppy ears.

It's a sight too nauseating to watch. Hattie gives Food Lady a quick peck on the cheek, and we dash upstairs to her room, just like always.

My hopes rise. Maybe he's stolen Hattie's heart, but I'm the one who'll be snuggling with her. She gets into her pajamas and disappears into the mint-smelling Bathtub Room. I curl up in the rumpled blankets, ready

for the cuddling and cooing and luxuriating in the soothing strokes of my hairbrush.

But when Hattie returns, she only brushes me a
couple of times before tossing the hairbrush onto the
chair. Is that it? No paw kissing? No "best buddies"
song? No snuggles?

I nose her arm, gazing up at her with my most irresist-
ibly cute face. But she's obviously still annoyed. Probably
because the barbecue wasn't any fun. She turns away.
Next thing I know, the room goes dark.

Later, when the whole house is still and quiet, Hattie
throws off the covers. "Shhh," she murmurs, and heads
for the door. After poking her head out, she tiptoes into
the hallway. Alone.

Where is she going? I sit with my head cocked,
watching the closed door and listening.

Soon I hear Hattie's quiet footsteps returning. My
tail wags with joy, until the door opens . . .

And the cage appears!

"Shhh," Hattie whispers. Holding her breath, she
sets the cage on the way-up-high dresser.

My tail sags. I should've known she'd bring him up
here. Pretty soon he'll be taking over the whole house.
And Hattie's whole life.

She reaches into the cage. Out comes the

trembling little fur ball cradled in Hattie's loving hands. "Thumper," she soothes, caressing his fur.

I sink into the rumpled blankets. I have to do something. If only I knew what.

After the enemy is back in his cage and Hattie's head is on the pillow, I nuzzle against her cheek. But it's impossible to sleep.

On top of the dresser, the Evil Bunny nestles into his rustle-y bed. Getting way too comfortable.

Goldie said this would happen. Whoa, was she ever right.

This is not the way bedtime's supposed to be. My gaze falls on the hairbrush lying on the chair. My heart swells with sadness.

Eventually, my eyelids get heavy . . .

At last! Hattie picks up the hairbrush. She brushes my coat and sings, "Best buddies, best buddies."

I cuddle against her shoulder, sighing with pure happiness. Everything's right again. Until a revolting stench assaults my nostrils.

It's that Evil Bunny! How did he get onto Hattie's pillow?

"Awww," Hattie coos, nuzzling his floppy ears. She starts stroking his nasty, bunny-ish fur. "Best buddies, best buddies," she sings to him!

He purrs with delight.

No! Hattie, no! I turn away, whimpering and shuddering . . .

And then, I'm someplace bright and sunny and grassy—outside in the Dog Park.

Hattie runs around, waving a stick. Her face is wide and smiling.

Hooray! Hooray! I love to play keep-away!

I rush over to her, ready for the chase, but she must not see me. She rushes right up to a floppy-eared fur ball, teasing him with the irresistible stick.

Before I can even react, the Evil Bunny scampers after her, his eyes full and gleaming. He clearly wants that stick.

Hattie giggles like crazy. She zigs and zags, the nasty creature chasing her around the Dog Park. *My Dog Park!*

Dog Parks are for dogs!

I race around, prepared to snatch that stick—and Hattie's attention—but no matter what I do or where I go, I can't get close enough.

All I can do is watch them romp through the grass, having the time of their lives. Until finally Hattie slows to a stop. Panting and laughing, she flops down in the grass.

The Evil Bunny hops onto her chest. She pulls him into her arms. Where she's holding a plump, glistening hot dog. With ketchup!

My tongue drips uncontrollably. *I need that hot dog! And*

my beloved Hattie! I start to run to her, but somehow I end up running in circles. I can't get near them!

Hattie grins. She wiggles the hot dog at the Evil Bunny.

His whiskers twitch. His mouth opens. His fang-like teeth go to chomp . . .

My eyes pop open. Hattie's room is filled with bright morning light. And I'm curled up beneath her chair.

I creep out for a stretch. And a look.

The Evil Bunny is rambling around the cage, perfectly at home on top of Hattie's dresser. And she's peacefully snoozing in her bed.

While her once-beloved dog is camped out on the floor.

It's every kind of wrong. I have to take action. Now. How hard can it be to scare off a bunny? After all, I chase squirrels for a living.

I leap onto the bed for a closer view. But there's a Very Big Problem. The cage that's keeping him trapped is also keeping him safe. Talk about a bad combination!

I'm going to need help. And I can't wait for the Evil Bunny Gang to come get him.

The blanket nudges my bum. "Fenway?" Hattie grumbles, her eyes fluttering awake.

My tail wags hopefully. I climb over the lumpy, bumpy covers to reach her. "I'm right here, Hattie," I bark. "Your adorable dog! Remember me?"

Hattie sits up and rubs her face. And then a *f-f-f-f-t!* noise drifts in through the window. She leans her elbows on the sill.

I jump up onto her lap, my nose pressing against the screen. The Dog Park below is quiet. And so is the one next door. Except ours is empty and the ladies' is not.

Goldie is in the far end of their Dog Park, chasing her tail. Patches bounds over and sinks low on her front paws, inviting Goldie to play. But when Goldie responds with a snap, Patches sulks off toward the bushes.

Angel plods into the grass, her arms bare, her cap on her head. She picks up her fat leathery glove and tosses the white ball way up high. And then . . . *thwap!* She snags it tight.

Hattie perks up. She turns, about to hop out of bed, when the *f-f-f-f-t!* sounds again. She returns to the window.

Zahra appears, wearing a cap like Angel's. Her long, silky hair swings like a tail behind her head. She bounces down the porch steps and joins Angel in the grass. "Hey!" she calls.

Hattie sucks in a breath.

Angel's hands fly to her hips. She yells at Zahra in a gruff voice. I catch one very clear word: "*Ript!*"

Whatever that means, Zahra doesn't like it. She shakes her head. "No!" she cries, her voice full of horror.

Angel's shoulders stiffen. She huffs at Zahra, more angry words spewing out of her mouth.

Smelling anxious, Hattie leans into the screen. She opens her mouth as if to call to them, but then she gulps like her words got stuck.

After a quick and irritated glance at me, she pauses. Her eyes remind me of a dog who's just spied an opportunity, like an unguarded bone.

We turn back to the window. Zahra continues shaking her head. "No," she keeps saying. She wipes her face. Finally, she turns and flies back up to the porch. Another *f-f-f-f-t!* and she's gone.

CHAPTER 14

Hattie sinks back on the bed, her eyes still big with that look of opportunity. She springs up and pulls on her clothes like she can't get them on fast enough. She grabs the cage and tiptoes downstairs, peering over her shoulder a whole bunch of times.

In the Eating Place, Hattie wolfs down a bowl of sloshy cereal at the counter. I keep an eye on my nemesis between licking drips off the floor. He glares back at me with those beady eyes. I will find a way to get rid of him if it's the last thing I do.

When Food Lady arrives and heads for the coffee-pot, Hattie wipes her mouth. She offers Food Lady an exaggerated grin. "See?" she says, stashing her bowl in the dishwasher.

Food Lady glances up from her steaming mug. She smiles as me and Hattie race to the back door.

Yippee! We're going outside! My tail goes nuts. "I'm so ready! I'm so ready!" I bark.

We bolt through the door, and I sniff the warm, sunshiny breeze. My ears rise at the sounds of jingling on the other side of the fence.

Hattie must hear it, too. She runs straight to the Friend Gate and pulls it open.

I leap and twirl. Hooray! Hooray! We're going to play!

We rush through the Friend Gate into the Dog Park next door. Hattie strides over to Angel, who's slumped on the porch steps. Her face is frowning and sad, like she's lost her favorite squeaky toy. When she sees Hattie, she crosses her arms.

I trot up to Goldie, and we do the bum-circle dance. She smells concerned. About Angel? "What's happening?" I ask.

"That's what I'd like to know," she says. "How's the bunny situation?"

My ears droop. "Rotten. I haven't made any progress at all."

"Hmm. Perhaps that's for the best," Patches says, wandering over. "You might want to rethink this. Thumper is new. He's probably scared. Maybe you could try being kind and patient with him."

"Oh, there goes Patches and her great advice," Goldie says with a huff. "Bunnies belong in the wild anyway. You'll be doing this guy a favor when you reunite him with that gang of his."

Patches gazes at me with pleading eyes. "Look, Fenway. I just think there could be another—"

"Stop it!" I shout at her. "I know you're on that Evil Bunny's side."

Patches recoils. "Believe it or not, I'm on your side," she mutters as she backs away.

Is she serious? Be kind and patient . . . with that nasty fur ball? She is clearly not the one looking out for me. I turn to Goldie. "Do you wish you'd gotten rid of Patches when you had the chance?"

"Now, don't go putting words in my mouth," she says.

"But she was so annoying. And ungrateful."

Goldie sighs. "Well, she didn't stay a puppy forever. Unlike your bunny, who will always be a bunny."

"You're right. He needs to leave." I sink down in the grass. "But there's a Very Big Problem."

Goldie's ears perk. "What's that?"

"The cage." I pause to think. And scratch under my bumpy collar. "It's trapping him in, but it's also keeping me out."

Goldie cocks her head. "Hmm, that does sound like a problem."

"You should see Hattie snuggle him," I say. "It's the very definition of revolting. What I need is a solution. And soon."

Goldie glances at Patches, who's now curled up in the grass. Then she faces me again, a strange gleam in her eye. "What was that you said about snuggling?"

My stomach clenches with the horrible memories. "Hattie pulls that Evil Bunny out of the cage, and—hey, wait a minute, Goldie!" I cry. "Are you saying . . . ?"

Goldie paws the ground. "Next time she does, you'll be ready for the chase?" she murmurs in a sly voice. "Could work."

"That's it!" I jump and spin. It's the Best Idea Ever! "Wowee! Thanks, Goldie! You're a real friend."

"Whoa, calm down there, Fenway," Goldie says. "Your victory hasn't happened yet."

I stop spinning. "But it's only a matter of time," I say, dropping down in the grass. "Now I have a great plan. Thanks to you."

She flops down beside me, her golden paw covering my brown one. "Your chance will come," she says. "And you'll be ready."

I look over at the short humans. Angel's still slumped on the step, her arms still folded. She grits her teeth. She says a word that I know, "Zahra," and one that I don't, "lied." It must mean something terrible, because Angel is mad and sad at the same time.

Hattie's gaze drifts to the ground. She and Angel are quiet for a few minutes. Hattie's forehead scrunches, like she's trying to think.

Then Hattie's eyebrows arch like she's got an idea. "Hey!" she pats Angel's shoulder. "See-Thumper?"

Angel's face brightens. "Okay," she says.

Hattie takes her hand. "Come on!"

I jump to my feet. "Did you hear that?" I say to Goldie. "They're probably headed for the cage! This could be my big opportunity!"

"Good luck," she calls.

"Fenway," Patches cries. "Maybe you should stop and think . . ."

I tune her out. The short humans make their way to the Friend Gate. I'm right on their heels, my tail going berserk. I'm so ready! I'm so ready!

Hattie babbles nonstop. "Thumper, Thumper," she says, her voice full and cheery. The short humans pick up speed as they skip through our Dog Park, up the porch steps, and into the house.

I'm practically romping on Hattie's sneakers. I have to stick by her side every second. My big chance is almost here!

Food Lady walks by, an overflowing basket of dirty clothes balanced on her hip. She greets Angel with a smile, then heads downstairs to the Musty-Smelling Place.

Hattie pulls Angel into the Eating Place. "Ta-da!" she says, going straight to the table. And the cage.

Angel leans in, her face glowing. "Aw," she coos. She wiggles her fingers at the Evil Bunny.

The second Hattie unlatches the door, I start leaping wildly. Whoopee! It's almost time for Goldie's plan!

Hattie shoves her arm inside the cage. She reaches for the nasty fur ball, who's huddled in the corner, trembling. And twitching with evil.

Sure enough, Hattie scoops him out, grinning proudly. She rubs his fur against Angel's cheek.

"Awww," Angel says again, caressing the Evil Bunny's back.

My fur ripples with disgust.

Hattie sucks in a breath. She smiles hopefully at Angel. "Fenway . . . park?" she asks, nuzzling her chin against the Evil Bunny's head.

My ears spike. Hattie's talking about me, and the park! But just as quickly, my ears flop with sadness. She might be talking about me, but she's nuzzling *him*.

Angel looks surprised. She glances at the door where Food Lady disappeared. "But—what?" she starts to ask.

Hattie doesn't let her finish. She thrusts the Evil Bunny into her hands.

Angel gasps. She gazes at the bunny adoringly. "Awww . . ."

I'm not exactly sure what's going on, except that the short humans are distracted. Which can only mean one thing—opportunity. I've never been more ready!

I leap up, throwing myself at Angel's legs. "Drop that bunny!"

She wobbles and grabs onto a chair to steady herself. "What the—?" she cries, her eyes wide and startled.

The Evil Bunny flies out of Angel's arms. He hops wildly around her legs. *Squeeeeeeeee! Squeeeeeeeee! Squeeeeeeeee!*

"Angel!" Hattie screams, pointing at the bunny.

Angel goes to nab him, but he squirts out of her grasp. "No!" she cries as he skitters under the chair.

I'm ready to pounce. "Surrender, bunny!" I bark. I lunge for his fluffy little tail, but he manages to hop out of reach.

Squeeeeeeeee! Squeeeeeeeee! Squeeeeeeeee!

"FEN-way!" Hattie yells, scrambling toward me.

The bunny scampers around a table leg, then rockets out of the room.

Squeeeeeeeee! Squeeeeeeeee! Squeeeeeeeee!

I burst into the hallway. "Do you think you can escape?"

Hattie races after us. "FEN-way!" she cries.

That Evil Bunny sure can fly! I follow him into the Lounging Place.

The short humans are hot on my tail. "FEN-way!" Hattie yells. "Stop!"

I zip around the couch and pull to a halt. How did I lose sight of that squealing little coward?

He can't have gotten far. Based on the bunny-ish stench, he's nearby. Nose to the ground, I sniff for clues.

I track the scent around the other side of the couch, my nostrils working overtime. The low table smells like books and magazines and flowers. The comfy chair smells like Food Lady and lemony tea. And the couch smells like Fetch Man's socks. Maybe that nasty fur ball's not on the furniture, but he's here somewhere. And I'm going to find him!

I circle past Angel, who's on her hands and knees, peeking under the couch.

Hattie rushes up behind me, her arms reaching . . .

Whew! I shoot behind the couch, barely beyond her grabby hands. She's trying to sabotage my efforts!

My nose leading the way, I follow the stinky trail

along the back of the couch. Yowza! He definitely went this way.

Angel's fingers nearly grab my hind paw, but I'm way too quick for her. I race to the other end of the couch. I should've known she'd take the bunny's side, too.

I'm diving under a small table when suddenly it teeters and—*crash!* A lamp falls and shatters on the floor.

"Oh no!" Hattie's jaw drops. So does Angel's.

Clearly, they were upset by the loud noise. But I can't let anything distract me! I speed around the table legs, hopping over jagged pieces of broken pottery. The scents are getting stronger. My nose is going wild. I'm getting closer to that Evil Bunny!

I rush past the low table, my hind leg bumping the corner with a *thump!* A vase of flowers wobbles, then— *smash! Splash!*

Water starts trickling off the low table. Flowers flop onto the floor. I barely dart out of the way in time.

"Get-im!" Hattie cries, pointing.

I'm about to leap onto a puffy chair when Angel comes at me from the other side. I pivot sharply and crawl underneath instead. It's dark and cramped and stuffy. The perfect place for a cowardly bunny to hide!

I smell him before I see him. When my eyes adjust

to the darkness, I'm face-to-face with the little monster himself!

"Ha! I've got you now!" I bark, lunging.

He rockets away, squealing hysterically. Like the coward he is.

I'm scootching after him, sounds of muffled gasps and short humans' footsteps all around. By the time I burst out from underneath the chair, Hattie's sweating and panting and searching under the couch. Angel's at her side, trying to catch her breath.

But there's no sign of that Evil Bunny. He's obviously hiding again.

Like he can get away with that. His scent can't hide!

Nose to the rug, I'm scooting past Hattie when her hand seizes my hind leg. "Hey, let me go!" I bark, kicking furiously. "I'm in the middle of a job!"

"FEN-way, stop!" Hattie shouts, clearly upset. Like she's the one whose plan got interrupted.

"Not now!" I bark. "I have an Evil Bunny to track!" I'm yelping and thrashing with all my might when Hattie's eyes widen in horror. And Food Lady screams.

Chapter 15

"Hattie!" Food Lady yells. Something terrible must've happened in the Musty-Smelling Place, because she sounds awfully upset. She gazes around the Lounging Place, her face horrified.

Did she have a plan that got interrupted, too?

Hattie exchanges a worried look with Angel. She smells scared. And anxious.

Food Lady's hands are on her hips. She glares at Hattie, clearly waiting for Hattie to say something.

But all Hattie can do is gulp.

It's obvious that more than one disaster is going on here. But I have to stay focused. "Outta my way, people!" I bark, kicking until my leg pulls free of Hattie's clutches. "I'm in the middle of an important job!"

"FEN-way!" Hattie screams. She lunges after me, but I'm way too speedy.

Sniffing wildly, I race over the rug, through broken pottery pieces, and around the puffy chair. That nasty creature thinks he can hide from this nose? Ha! He's dealing with a professional! He's definitely somewhere in the Lounging Place, and I won't rest until I find him.

"FEN-way!" Hattie rushes across the room, making a wide arc around the low table. She's trying to head me off!

"Nice try, Hattie!" I shoot out of her grasp in the nick of time. Me and Hattie have played chase so many times, I know all her moves. There's no way she can catch me.

I hop around a soggy magazine, over the limp flowers, and take a sharp turn toward the couch.

Food Lady lets out an angry sigh. "Hattie, what . . . ?"

I catch a fresh whiff of bunny under one end of the couch. I dive into the darkness.

"Angel!" Hattie shouts. I hear short human footsteps run up behind me. Another set rush over to the other end of the couch.

"I-got-im!" Angel's voice cries. Next thing I know, her sideways face appears up ahead of me.

Hattie's guarding one potential exit, while Angel's patrolling another. It's the oldest trick in the history of chase. Do they think I'm an amateur? I halt in my tracks and poke my head out from under the middle of the couch.

Just then, Fetch Man charges in from the Dog Park, reeking of oil. "What the—?" he cries. "Hattie?"

Food Lady pivots. "Oh no!" she shouts, her eyes full of horror. She rushes toward him, pointing at the dark, greasy footprints trailing behind Fetch Man.

Yippee! A distraction! I squirt out from under the couch, my nose tracking the odious bunny scent.

"Angel!" Hattie yells as I zoom around Angel's sneakers.

I'm vaguely aware of Angel's reaching hands, but I've got something more important to focus on. The odor is overwhelming. And the drapes are twitching . . .

Just as Angel's fingers start to close around me, I spurt out and zip over to those drapes! I root under the heavy fabric, my nose assaulted by the stench—aha! I'm ready to pounce!

Squeeeeeee! Squeeeeeee! Squeeeeeee! The Evil Bunny scampers past me and shoots out from under the drapes.

Why, that little—! I race after him, just as the fur ball flies toward Angel. Her grabby hands are about to nab him.

"Angel!" Hattie screams. "Get-im!"

"What?" Fetch Man and Food Lady yell at the same time, frozen. Their faces have matching expressions of shock.

Angel lunges for the Evil Bunny. Her fingers brush his hind leg, but he tears away and scampers out of the Lounging Place before she can grab him. She shrieks and bolts after him. Hattie's not far behind.

The short humans are fast, but I'm faster. I bolt past them down the hallway, hot on that bunny's evil, cottony tail. "You think you can outrun me?" I bark.

Squeeeeeee! Squeeeeeeee! Squeeeeeeee! He heads straight for the back door. That's partially open.

"Prepare for certain doom!" I bark. I'm hauling as fast as I can, but the Evil Bunny gets to the door first . . .

And shoots outside!

I'm about to rocket after him, but Hattie's hands close around my torso. Talk about bad timing! "What'd you do that for?" I bark, twisting and squirming. "I almost had him!"

But as usual, Hattie doesn't get it. She thrusts me into Fetch Man's greasy hands as she, Angel, and Food Lady speed past us and out the door.

Fetch Man sets me down. "Stay!" he yells, then races out the door himself.

I bound after him, but he slides the door shut. Practically on my snout! "Hey!" I bark, scratching the screen. But it's no use. They're all out in the Dog Park except me. Even the Evil Bunny!

All I can do is watch. But there's no sign of that nasty creature anywhere.

The humans are all frantic. And busy. Hattie and Angel zigzag across the porch, bending and craning their heads under the table and chairs. Food Lady investigates a pile of tools scattered in the grass. She studies the quiet lawn mower and peeks in its grassy bag. Fetch Man searches beneath the barbecue.

After scouring every inch of the porch, Hattie and Angel rush around the Dog Park. Their heads swivel aimlessly as if they can't make up their minds where to look.

Food Lady checks out the vegetable patch. Fetch Man examines the lawn mower bag, even though Food Lady's already looked there. Angel drops to her hands and knees and peeks under the bushes, while Hattie races to the giant tree.

She scales the ladder-y steps up the trunk and disappears in the leafy branches. Soon the upper half of her body pokes out the window of the little house. Her head twists from side to side, her hand shielding her eyes. She gazes into the Dog Park below like she's looking for a lost bone. Or a ball.

Fetch Man and Food Lady head to the Friend Gate.

Fetch Man gives it a rattly pull and seems glad that it's shut tight. The tall humans walk slowly and carefully around the perimeter of the whole Dog Park. When they get to the back fence behind the giant tree, Fetch Man squats on his haunches. He examines a patch of dirt, bending his head way down. Is he trying to see under the fence? Hey, is that the spot where the Evil Bunny Gang's hole was before?

Food Lady crouches next to Fetch Man. She looks under the fence, too. Even from the house, I can see the distress on their faces.

When Hattie finally climbs down from the giant tree, she and Angel gather with the tall humans around the hole. They are huddled together, staring at it like it's the most interesting thing they've ever seen.

If only I weren't trapped behind the door, I'd be all over that hole. What if the Evil Bunny Gang is on the other side, growling and thumping their sinister hind legs? Or coming for their leader after all?

Hey, wait a minute! I've been so focused on watching the humans, I almost forgot that I haven't seen one single trace of that Evil Bunny this entire time. Where is he?

My heart races with the amazing thought . . .

The Evil Bunny is not in the Dog Park because he is GONE!

CHAPTER 16

Hooray! Hooray! I leap and twirl for joy.
The Evil Bunny is gone! I knew Goldie's idea would
work. It was the Best Idea Ever!

Now we can go back to how things are supposed
to be. I'm so excited, I can hardly control myself. But
then I hear Hattie's voice yelling, and I stop mid-romp.
What's going on?

Hattie's in the middle of the Dog Park. Her face is
angry. Her arms are flailing. She's growling at Angel.

Angel's shoulders slump. Her eyes are sad and wet.
She sniffs and snorts, chattering back at Hattie.

Hattie is really mad. She's yelling sounds like "Yew-did-it" and "Yew-dropt-im!" and "Yew-let-im-get-awaaaaay!" Her forehead scrunched up, she keeps shouting at Angel until Fetch Man rushes over. He clamps a hand on Hattie's arm.

Tears glisten on Angel's cheeks. Fetch Man starts to talk to her, his eyes full of kindness, but she turns and flees through the Friend Gate.

As Angel hurries off, Hattie breaks into sobs. Fetch Man puts his arm around her heaving shoulders.

Apparently Hattie doesn't want to be comforted. She shrugs out of his grasp, clenching her fists. What made Hattie so mad? The Evil Bunny running away? Why is she mad at Angel?

One thing's for sure—Hattie is upset. But luckily, she's got her beloved and loyal dog to cheer her up.

And she must be thinking the exact same thing. Her face angry, her nose sniffling, she sprints through the grass right toward me. My tail goes into auto-wag mode.

She races up the steps, flies across the porch, and slides the door open.

"I'm so glad you're back, Hattie," I bark. "Let's play!" I chomp a squeaky toy and bounce on my paws, gazing up at her invitingly.

Hattie sucks in a breath. She shakes a finger at me. "Bad boy! Bad boy!" she yells. She sounds furious.

Whoa! Her anger is too painful to bear. My ears sag. My tail slumps. I drop the squeaky toy. I slink back.

Hattie keeps shaking that angry finger. Her voice rises with even more fury. "Bad! Bad! Bad!" she shouts.

I sink down on the floor and turn my head. Maybe if I don't look at her, if I don't listen, it won't hurt so much.

Hattie's yelling turns into sobbing. And hiccuping. Finally, she flies down the hall. I hear her footsteps bounding up the stairs.

My heart shatters. Why didn't I see this coming? She's gone. And I'm alone with the terrible truth—

Hattie doesn't love me anymore.

I'm curled up for a Long, Long Time.

I thought Hattie loving that Evil Bunny was the worst thing that could happen. But that's nothing compared to the horribly sick feeling in my tummy right now.

Why did she stop loving me? Wasn't I cute and cuddly? Wasn't I fun to play with? Didn't I do a good enough job of making her happy?

My body's so heavy, I can't even move. Not that I'd want to. Without Hattie, what would I even do?

Chapter 17

A familiar sound wakes me. *F-f-f-f-t!* **The** sliding door closes. Fetch Man and Food Lady come in from the porch. Their heads are hung. Their faces are pained. They smell helpless and frustrated.

I know how they feel.

Fetch Man sighs and wraps his arm around Food Lady's shoulder. If they notice the poor, pathetic dog curled up in the corner, they don't let on. They plod into the Eating Place and slump around the table. With the empty cage. They chatter in low voices, sounding concerned.

Soon I hear Hattie's footsteps padding down the stairs. She strides into the Eating Place, too. Fetch Man pats the seat beside him, and she plops onto it.

Hattie's eyes are puffy. She rests her chin in her hands. She listens as Fetch Man speaks in a serious voice.

When he finishes speaking, she springs out of her seat. Her face is pleading. Her lower lip is trembling. "Keep-ser-ching!" she says. She sounds desperate. She starts to move to the back door.

I push up onto my paws. I creep closer.

Fetch Man cocks his head. "Hattie . . ." he calls.

Just then—*vroooooooom!*

The noise drifts in from the front windows. Everyone freezes.

Across the street, a car door slams.

Hattie gasps. "Oh no!" she cries. She races to the front of the house.

I slink into the hallway for a better look. Hattie's peering out the window. At Whisker Face and Round Lady's house. Her hands fly to her face.

Fetch Man and Food Lady rush to Hattie's side. They all hold a shared breath, standing still for a moment, gaping across the street like they can't believe their eyes.

Hattie's the first to turn away. Her face is full of panic. "Now-what?" she sobs.

Food Lady rubs Hattie's arm. Fetch Man speaks to her in a sober voice. It's obvious they're both trying to calm her. And it's not working.

Hattie clenches her fists. She bounces up and down.

"No . . . no!" she shouts, her nose sniffling, her face frantic with fear. She shirks away from the tall humans and tears down the hall.

What could be so scary? I don't hear any loud booming noises. I don't smell fire or smoke. But something terrifying must be happening, because Hattie is really afraid.

I run into the Eating Place and leap onto her legs. "Whatever it is, let me handle it," I bark. "I'm your protector."

"FEN-way," she snaps. She grabs me by my new collar and holds me at arm's length. "Stop it!"

"Hattie, I can help," I bark, straining to get loose. "If you'd let me." I pull and pull. I'm desperate to jump into her arms—*fwoop!*

Ha! I've slipped right out of the collar. I throw myself at her.

"FEN-way!" she scolds, turning away with a huff. She goes over to the tall humming box and pulls the door open. A burst of cold air wafts out.

I move closer, my tail wagging. As if there were any hope she'd be getting us some yummy ice cream. Or a hot dog.

Hattie grabs a big pointy carrot and closes the humming box. With a loud breath, she heads out the back door. It's clear she's going outside, armed with that carrot. She probably wants to find a new Evil Bunny to love.

I heave an enormous sigh. Why can't she love just me? I'm her beloved dog. I snuggle with her. I play with her. I make her happy.

What does she need an Evil Bunny for?

I curl up on the floor. Trapped. Alone. And rejected. I'm about to close my eyes again when I see a flicker of dazzling light.

My sparkly collar.

I get up and skulk over to it. It's lying limp on the floor, glittering. I bat it with my paws.

I hate that collar. It's bumpy and itchy. And I already have a perfectly good collar. One that jingles. What did Goldie say . . . that it wasn't my style? Ha!

I growl at that stupid collar. Hattie made it for me back when she loved me and adored me and fussed over me. But then that bunny came and she just stopped.

Snarling, I bear down on my front paws. I open my mouth. I pounce!

Chomp! Take that, you annoying collar! I never liked you anyway. I step my brown paw onto one end. My jaws tear at the other. It tastes like string and plastic. Yuck!

I won't be deterred! I drive my claws into another spot on the sparkly collar. I bite the beads and string, pulling with all my might.

Bits of gritty glitter fly out of my mouth. I want to gag, but I won't stop. Not until the sparkly collar is destroyed once and for all!

Me and Hattie were happy before those Evil Bunnies came. Why did they have to ruin everything?

Chomp! Pull! *R-r-r-r-r-rip!* Patooey!

Beads clatter and roll and scatter on the floor. You get what you deserve, sparkly collar!

And what about Goldie? Chasing away the Evil Bunny was all her idea. And look at the good it did me! The bunny's gone and Hattie doesn't love me anymore. Some friend Goldie turned out to be. She gave me the Worst Idea Ever! Next time I see her, I'll—I'll—

I grab hold of what's left of the sparkly collar. *Chomp!* I tug and tug and—*r-r-r-r-rip!* More sparkly beads fall off. More shreds of soggy string cling to my mouth. I gag.

What did Hattie see in that Evil Bunny anyway? What's so lovable about him? He's a nasty and annoying creature. All he did was huddle in a cage. Rustling in the hay. And twitching those evil whiskers. What was that all about?

He never snuggled on her pillow. Or played fetch. Or protected her from danger!

Chomp! Pull! *R-r-r-r-r-rip!* The sparkly collar is nothing but shreds dangling from a metal clasp.

Glittery beads are sprinkled all over the floor. It's officially destroyed. I gag a few more times. At least one job is done.

I drink long, sloppy, throat-clearing gulps from my water dish. The used-to-be collar betrayed me. The Evil Bunny stole my short human. Patches wasn't on my side. Goldie didn't help me at all. And Hattie stopped loving me.

I'm mad at everybody! And everything! I'm the Maddest Dog Ever!

I'm searching the Eating Place for another victim . . . a broom? a dish towel? . . . when the door slides open, and Hattie trudges in. With the carrot.

She's sobbing uncontrollably. She's completely dejected. Her face is full of pain, like she wants to melt away and never come back.

My heart is crushed all over again.

CHapter 18

My Hattie is miserable. And there's nothing I can do about it.

Well, maybe there's one thing . . . but it might be too big, even for a professional like me.

Anyway, I can't do anything stuck in here. "Please . . . oh, please . . . somebody please let me out . . ." I whine, pawing furiously at the door. I whimper. I howl. It's an emergency!

I hear Hattie's footsteps pad up the stairs, then fade away. I keep at it. "I can't wait even one more second . . ." I cry, louder and more urgently this time. "I have to go ooooooouuuuuuut!"

It takes a couple more moans and howls, but eventually it works! Fetch Man rushes in from the

Lounging Place holding a rattly garbage bag. His face is all business. "Let's go, Fenway," he says with an exasperated sigh.

"I'm so ready! I'm so ready!" I bark, jumping up and down. Fetch Man opens the door and I trot onto the porch.

Now what?

I peer up at a dark, gloomy cloud rolling across the sky. I sniff the heavy, rushing breeze. I scan the Dog Park, shivering.

Plants and shrubs wave in the wind. The leafy leaves in the giant tree ripple and swoosh. Even the low branches are creaking and swaying.

My ears perked, I listen to the breeze whistling and sobs coming down from Hattie's window.

My heart is overcome with sadness. My legs feel heavy, stuck in place.

I turn my snout into the whooshing wind again. My coat ripples and ruffles. I can't just stand here.

I give myself a good shake. And just like that, I snap out of my misery. It's up to me to make Hattie happy. It might mean giving my nemesis what he wants, but I'm tough enough to take it.

There's no other way. I must find that Evil Bunny! I have to save him and bring him back to Hattie.

I trot through the grass, my ears alert, my snout

sniffing and swiveling. Clues are here somewhere and I will find them!

I'm checking out the bushes when I notice a slight rustle. A furry little swish? It's the Evil Bunny! I'd know him anywhere.

Like a shot, I dive under the fluttering bush. It smells odious all right! I crawl deeper under the bushy branches until a sickening sound freezes me in my tracks.

Chipper. Chatter. Squawk!

I back out into the grass. A few bushes down, a small head pops out of the shrubby leaves. A bristly tail flounces. A twig snaps.

My hackles pricked, I prepare my most menacing growl. How dare that squirrel barge into the Dog Park! Especially at a time like this!

"The Dog Park is for dogs!" I bark, racing after him.

Rustle. Crackle. Swish. The squirrel scampers up the bush and flings himself onto the fence.

I leap up and paw the fence. I'm about to give him the business when another horrifying sight comes into view. Another squirrel appears right next to the first one. Where did he come from?

Two against one is hardly a fair fight. Especially when they have a significant height advantage over me. I slink back, squinting into the wind. "You're a couple of . . . c-c-cowards!" I bark.

Chipper. Chatter. Squawk! The squirrels peer down from the fence top, taunting. Jeering.

My fur prickles. "I'm warning you for the last . . . t-t-time!" I bark, glancing up at the threatening cloud. Which is somehow way bigger than it was a second ago.

The squirrels go on chippering at me. Shuddering, I take another backward step. I didn't come out here to mess with a gang of squirrels! I have a job to do. What is it about those nasty creatures, anyway? Why are they so horribly annoying? And distracting?

Intruding where they don't belong, twittering and chittering, taunting. Just asking to be chased. Or worse.

My gaze locked with their beady little eyes, I continue backing away. They're no match for a vicious dog like me. They're nothing but cowards!

The Evil Bunnies are the biggest cowards of all. With their terrifying leg thumps, their ear-splitting squeals, their horrifying chomping teeth—not to mention their stench! I tremble just remembering the first time I smelled it.

I'm backing up some more when my hind paw hits a wobbly wire fence. The vegetable patch where that first Evil Bunny prowled through. Clearly one of the gang! He ate the lettuce and the vegetables. Before I tracked him to that hole under the back fence . . .

The back fence!

I look past the giant tree to the back of the Dog Park. Is that the same hole? The one that smelled like bunnies?

Whooooooooooooo . . . whooooooooo . . . the thick wind whistles. How did the sky get so dark? It's the middle of the daytime.

With every bit of fur on my back bristling with fear—I mean, courage—I creep over to investigate. I paw the dirt, sniffing around the edges. That hole smells bunny-ish all right.

My paws are slow and shaky. I inch closer. I poke my snout into the hole. *Sniff . . . sniff . . .* the Evil Bunny odor is everywhere. But it's not very strong.

Which can only mean one thing—the bunny, or bunnies, are someplace else.

I whip my head around, frantically searching the Dog Park again. So where did they go?

Whooooooooooooo . . . whooooooooo . . . the wind howls. Its voice is sultry. And menacing. A bad combination.

Whoa. I huddle against the fence, my fur matted back in the breeze. My eyes adjusting to the strange darkness. My body trembling with . . . anticipation.

I squint into the wind. Hunting bunnies is a dangerous job. But no crying wind or dark sky or chippering squirrels will stop me. I have to save Hattie from misery! Nothing has ever been more important.

Nose to the ground, I zigzag through the grass. I

catch whiffs of Fetch Man and Food Lady, Hattie and Angel . . . and every now and then, I pick up the stench of bunny . . . one . . . two . . . how many are there? I quake with confidence. The trail leads somewhere. And I won't rest until the nasty end!

I sniff my way along the side fence, the wind fierce and rushing into my face. As I approach the Friend Gate, I gaze up and halt in my tracks.

What's this? The Friend Gate is opening. Is somebody coming? I wait and wait. But nobody appears. How is the Friend Gate opening by itself?

My fur standing on end, I trot up to it. Right into a powerful gust of wind.

As the Friend Gate swings wider and wider and wider, I crane my head. My neck swiveling on high alert.

But all I see is grass. Nobody's there.

Whoooooooooooooo . . . whoooooooo . . . the wind wails. The Friend Gate starts to slap back.

Whoa! I jump out of the way just in time.

Smack! The Friend Gate bangs shut.

I thrust my snout under the gate, sniffing wildly. How did it open and close by itself? And more important, what's that smell?

My nose sniffing like crazy, I take whiffs of bunny after bunny after bunny. There's no question—the gang's all here.

I jerk back, shuddering. The evidence is solid all right. And terrifying.

But I have to go for it. Hattie's happiness is at stake!

Summoning all my bravery, I rush up to the Friend Gate again. My nose searches under, around, and up. What's this? A gap! The gate's not closed all the way.

I wiggle my snout into the gap, grunting and pushing, the heavy Friend Gate starting to budge. And then . . . it finally flies open!

I burst into the Dog Park next door. That Evil Bunny Gang is here. I know it! My expert nose will hunt them down!

I race through the grass, my nose leading the way. At first, I'm bombarded with scents of Angel, Goldie, and Patches . . . but every now and then I catch the faint scent of bunnies. I'm on the right track.

Whoooooooooooooo . . . whooooooooo . . . a gust of wind beats into my ears. Along with a familiar jingling sound. I turn toward it.

"Fenway!" Goldie lopes over, her tail wagging happily like nothing is wrong. "What's going on?"

"What's going on?" I repeat with a snarl. "Hattie's hurting and it's all your fault!"

Goldie freezes, her eyes glaring. "How is that?"

"You and your bad ideas," I growl. "The Evil Bunny's gone and everything is ruined."

Goldie humphs. "Well, if you ruined everything, that's not my problem."

Figures she'd say that. "Leave me alone, Goldie!" I say, baring my teeth. "I'm on an important mission and I don't need any more help from you!"

"That's fine with me!" she says, clearly miffed.

As she heads across the Dog Park, I notice Patches curled up near the back fence. She looks as miserable as the rest of us.

How can the ladies lounge around when there's an Evil Bunny Gang on the loose? Are they not aware of the stench?

Nose back to the ground, I follow a winding scent trail to the tangly vines next to the house. Aha!

Those vines are reeking with bunny smells! My tail going nuts, I thrust my snout into the web of jumbly twists. Furiously, I burrow and thrash. I push through snaky vines.

But the vines are empty. Where did the bunnies go?

I track the stench along the back of the house. When I reach the side of the porch, there's just enough space for me to crawl underneath.

And as my eyes adjust to the blackness, two glowing eyes beam back at me.

Chapter 19

My nose picks it up first. That stench of fear and aggression and rotten carrots is unmistakable! I'm staring into the face of my rival—

The Evil Bunny!

He's huddled in the corner, glowering at me. His body is poised and ready to strike.

My hackles shoot up with rage and loathing. Our eyes lock and horrible memories come back to me. The menacing taunts. The horrific rustling and scratching. The annoying carrot munching and chomping. The ear-splitting squeals and shrieks.

The fact that he stole my short human away from me.

I bare my teeth. "You're out of chances, bunny!" I bark.

He growls. He flinches. He's about to pounce!

I start to lunge—but I immediately pull back, my heart flooded with confusion and panic. I want to chase him away. But that's not why I tracked him down.

The Evil Bunny twitches, his wicked eyes darting one way, then the other. His whole body is trembling. He's obviously terrified—hey, what's that horrible smell?

My head swivels, and I leap back in horror. Through the darkness, more eyes are glowing with evil. Furry heads, twitching noses, great big teeth!

It's another nasty fur ball . . . and another . . . and another. Wowee, they are everywhere! It's the Evil Bunny Gang!

Is this their lair?

Every one of them is staring at me with looks of pure intimidation. And they clearly mean business! I take a step back, shivering with courage, trying to summon a growl, when . . .

Squeeeee!

I turn back to the Evil Bunny—Thumper. He is cowering in the corner, obviously terrified of the Evil Bunny Gang.

My eyes refocus. This little quivering fur ball isn't trouble. He's IN trouble.

And that's when I know I was wrong.

"Thumper" doesn't mean *Leader of the Bunny Gang*. Goldie was right—Thumper is his name. And it means *alone and afraid*. He needs help.

Thump! Thump! Thump!

Yikes! One of the bunnies stomps his chubby hind leg so loudly, so defiantly, my ears fight like crazy to stay upright. I can't move. I can't think. All I can do is shudder.

Another bunny opens his mouth. *Eeeeeeeeeeeee!* Some are shrieking and growling at Thumper. The rest are getting ready to pounce in my direction.

My ears fall in defeat. Who knew bunnies could be so loud? The gang is ganging up on me.

I creep backward, trying to stare them all down at the same time. I have a job to do, but this is not a fair fight. I can't conquer a whole Gang of Evil Bunnies on my own. I need reinforcements.

I back all the way out from under the porch and into the wind. *Whoooooooooo . . . whoooooooooo . . .* it howls.

My eyes squint into the rushing gust. My ears blown flat, my fur rippling, I sprint across the ladies' Dog Park.

Goldie's slumped down in the grass, her face in her paws. She barely looks up as I approach.

"Goldie! I need help! It's urgent!" I shout, nudging her until she meets my gaze.

She sneers. "Go away."

She's obviously mad that I blamed her for the mess I'm in. Somehow I have to convince her to forgive me before it's too late. "I'm sorry I yelled at you. But everything's changed!" I dart back and forth, my tail going nuts. "I found Thumper! He's under the porch."

"Good for you," she gruffs. "So get rid of him. Get your short human back. Have a nice life."

More darkness blankets the sky. Another gust of wind hits my face. *Whooooooooooo . . . whooooooooooo . . .* it moans.

"No—listen!" I plead. "He's in danger. I need help! And there's not much time!"

Patches trots over, her sleek fur even sleeker in the wind. "What is it, Fenway?" she asks, her face serious and concerned. "How can we help?"

Her voice is so lovely. Her eyes are so kind. Even though I was mean to her, she still wants to help. What a true friend. "Oh, Patches!" I cry, nuzzling her neck.

"He asked me, not you," Goldie snaps at her. "What help could you possibly be anyway? You're a total softy."

I turn to face Goldie, whose expression is even tougher and more growly than usual. "I have a plan. And I need you both."

Goldie snarls at Patches, clearly unconvinced. "Well, if she's helping, I have something better to do."

"Goldie, please!" I cry. "You're my friend. I need you."

She turns back to me. "That's my point. You need me, not her."

"We have to work together. As a pack! And we have to hurry."

Patches offers Goldie a look full of hope.

Goldie sighs.

Whoooooooooo . . . whoooooooooo . . . the wind whistles in my ears. I sprint back to the house. "Come on, ladies!" I call. "Let's go!"

For a few moments, all I hear is the wind. But then . . . tags jingling?

I look out into the Dog Park. The ladies are headed my way! I give a quick sniff under the porch. Eeeeew! "Good! They're still in there," I say.

"They?" Patches asks.

"The Evil Bunny Gang," I explain. "We're outnumbered."

Goldie cocks her head. "You don't seriously expect us to fit under there."

"Hold on, Goldie," Patches says. "What's the plan, Fenway?"

"All right, ladies. Listen up." As I dole out assignments, their heads nod in agreement. When we're all on board with the plan, we bump noses. "I owe you big-time," I whisper. We take our positions.

I crawl under the porch, my fur bristling with nerves—I mean, readiness. Through the empty black silence, the Evil Bunnies' glowing eyes—and their stench—betray them. Teeth bared and ready, I zero in on the gang.

Some rustling comes first, then *Squeeeeeeeee! Squeeeeeeeee! Squeeeeeeeee!*

I jump back in terror. Their shrieks are way louder than I expected! Quaking and trembling, I remind myself of the mission. I must prevail!

My back to Thumper, I bear down and prepare to attack. "You cannot escape, bunnies!" I bark, snarling and snapping and lunging.

Squeeeeeeeee! Squeeeeeeeee! Squeeeeeeeee! The Evil Bunnies all squeal at once, each headed toward the dim light of the opening. Where the ladies are waiting.

The gang rockets out, while Thumper huddles in the corner. I watch Patches get into position to block Thumper, then I head after the rest.

"That's it, cowards!" I bark. "Run for your lives!"

The squealing bunnies scamper past a growling Goldie. We chase their fluffy white tails, driving them across the grass.

Through the screaming, whining wind, I hear Patches's lovely voice behind me. "Aw, you poor dear. It's going to be okay now . . ."

Thumper's shrieks are getting quieter and quieter. I knew Patches could soothe him. The plan is working!

"Goldie . . . to the gate!" I shout, beginning to pant as we gain ground on the gang.

"Got it, boss!" Looking as tough as ever, she gallops toward the Friend Gate. It's swinging and banging in the vicious wind.

Squeeeeeeeee! Squeeeeeeeeee! Squeeeeeeeeee! The bunnies scurry through the grass in a frenzied effort to escape.

"Scram, you Evil Bunnies!" I bark, herding them toward Goldie.

Whooooooooooo . . . whooooooooooo . . . cries the wind, whooshing in my ears. A fat raindrop splashes on my nose.

"Go, Fenway, go!" Goldie calls, poised and ready to steady the gate.

"I'm . . . coming!" I yell, my tongue lolling, my sides heaving. Those bunny tails are mere inches from my mouth. I can practically taste them!

Through the fence, I hear the sound I've been waiting for. *F-f-f-f-t!*

"It's time! It's time!" I shout.

In one swift motion, Goldie springs up, her front paws pushing on the Friend Gate. With a squeaky creak, it swings wide. Goldie bolts through, her body leaning against the open gate.

The Evil Bunny Gang rushes through the Friend Gate, my teeth snapping behind them.

Goldie races after us, the gate banging shut behind her. "Not bad!" she cries.

"Awesome!" I yell with a quick glance at the porch. Sure enough, Hattie is there! My snout motions toward the middle of the Dog Park. "Goldie . . . go that way!"

"Fenway? Goldie?" Hattie's voice screams through the monstrous wind. When she spies the Evil Bunny Gang, her eyes nearly pop out of her head. She scrambles down the porch steps, obviously frantic.

"Don't worry, Hattie!" I bark. "I've got it all under control!" Or at least I hope I do.

Me and Goldie cut across the grass. I come at the bunnies from one direction, and Goldie comes from the other. "Get lost or prepare for certain doom, bunnies!" I bark. Another fat raindrop hits me in the eye.

Squeeeeeeeee! Squeeeeeeeee! Squeeeeeeeee! Shrieking with panic, they weave a crisscross path through the Dog Park, heading for the giant tree. They're fast for bunnies, but they're no match for a team like us.

The Friend Gate screeches open again. Angel dashes in, her face full of alarm. "Stop, Goldie! Stop!" she screams.

"Fenway!" Hattie cries. She rushes toward me and Goldie as we close ranks on the squealing bunnies.

"Goldie!" I shout, cocking my head toward the giant tree. "Over there!"

Goldie makes a wide arc around the frenzied bunnies as I chase them from the other side. We drive them through the Dog Park, past the giant tree, and over to the back fence. And the hole.

Whooooop! The first bunny dives into the hole, his bobbing white tail disappearing under the back fence. He's gone!

"One down, the rest to go!" I cry. Goldie growls. I snarl and snap. One by one, the rest of the Evil Bunny Gang shoots through the hole. The last one vanishes just as Hattie races around the giant tree.

"Fenway!" Hattie calls, her eyes wide and afraid. She drops to her knees and peers through the hole.

"Come on, Goldie!" I cry.

Goldie follows me back across the Dog Park and up to the Friend Gate.

"Hurry!" I shout.

Angel's right behind us. "Goldie!" she yells.

Goldie noses the gate open and swings it wide. I lead the way to the porch, where Patches is waiting, calm as can be. "How . . . is he?" I ask, panting. Me and the ladies sink onto our bellies and peer underneath the porch.

"Poor little guy," Patches says. "I did my best. But he's still a bit frightened."

As heavy sheets of rain begin pouring down, Angel arrives, huffing and puffing. She squats down beside us, smelling curious.

Squeeeeeeeee!

"What the—?" Angel peeks under the porch. And her mouth drops open.

Chapter 20

Angel drops to her belly. She stretches an arm way under the porch. "Awww," she coaxes. When she pulls her arm out, she's clutching Thumper.

Me and the ladies sit up tall, our tails thumping in approval.

"You did it, Fenway," Patches says.

"You mean, *we* did it," I correct. "But there's still one thing left."

I rush to the Friend Gate just as—

Cr-r-r-r-r-ack! BOOM-KABOOM! My eyes squint into a blanket of rain. I shiver with the rush of victory.

As soon as I reach the gate—*creak!* Hattie barrels through, wind whipping through her bushy hair.

"Great news, Hattie!" I bark, leading her to the porch.

"Fenway—what?" she shouts, racing behind me. And then—"Oh!" she gasps.

Even with wet hair blowing across her face, Angel's gigantic smile shines through. She offers Thumper to Hattie like a present.

"Oh! Oh!" Hattie cries again. She snatches the little fur ball and cuddles him under her chin. Her grin is as wide as her whole face. She is happy. Hattie is happy.

Through the blustery wind, my heart swells with warmth. "Check it out," I say to the ladies.

"Nice job," Patches says, visibly impressed.

Goldie gazes at me, her fur soggy and matted down. "Are you sure this is what you want?"

"Hattie's happiness is all that matters," I say.

Patches nuzzles my neck. "You're some dog, Fenway."

Aw, shucks.

Hattie strokes Thumper's back as Angel speaks to her in an excited voice. My ears perk when she says "Fenway" over and over. She must be talking about me because she's looking at me the entire time.

Hattie's face brightens with amazement. "Fenn-waay!" she cries, her voice full of gratitude. And devotion.

I rush to her side, my whole body wagging with joy. Hattie bends down and curls an arm around me. "Oh, Fenway," she coos, snuggling into my wet fur. "Good boy!"

That night, me and Hattie cuddle in her rumpled blankets. I cozy up in her lap, luxuriating in the familiar scent of mint and vanilla. And Hattie's love.

She kisses my brown paw, then my white paw. She showers my neck with kisses. "Best buddies, best buddies," she sings. She grabs the bedtime hairbrush and starts stroking my fur.

Ahhhh, that's the spot. I melt into a puddle of pure bliss. Until—

Scri-i-itch . . . scri-i-itch . . .

My ears cringe at the irritating sound. I gaze at the cage on top of the dresser. Thumper scrapes his teeth against the metal bars.

I actually feel sorry for him. Even though Fetch Man and Food Lady let Hattie bring him upstairs, he's trapped in that boring old cage while I get to snuggle with her all night. He's still alone. But at least he's safe. He must be awfully grateful I rescued him from the Evil Bunny Gang. Those bunnies were definitely trouble. If I hadn't showed up, who knows what could've happened?

"Best buddies, best buddies," Hattie sings. She smells

like the happiest short human in the world. All because of her loyal dog.

As she brushes my belly, I sigh contentedly. My hind leg kicks with delight. Me and Hattie are together, and nobody—not even an Evil Bunny—will ever come between us again.

When the window is just starting to get light, we hear *scri-i-itch . . . scri-i-itch . . . scri-i-itch . . .*

My ears spike. One eye pops open. Doesn't that bunny ever sleep?

Scri-i-itch . . . scri-i-itch . . .

Hattie groans and pulls the blanket over our heads. I cuddle against her shoulder.

When we finally get up, Hattie peeks quickly into the cage. She tugs her clothes on and whispers to him in a voice that's both sincere and hopeful.

Thumper doesn't even look at her. He's munching the hay, obviously not listening. Even though I saved him, he's probably still upset about what happened.

I paw the dresser, looking up at the cage. "It's okay, buddy," I bark. And somehow I know it will be.

After breakfast, me and Hattie bolt back upstairs. She grabs the cage and carefully carries it through the hall and down the stairs. She's all business, like she's got a destination in mind. I can hardly wait to see where we're going.

Fetch Man's putting on his shoes by the front door. Food Lady joins him, smelling awfully excited.

"Hooray! Hooray!" I bark, leaping and spinning. "We're going for a walk!"

Fetch Man opens the door, but Hattie stops him. "Fenway?" she says, nodding at my leash.

With a halfhearted shrug at Food Lady, he clips it onto my collar.

We head through sloshy puddles down the walkway and across the street. And right away, I notice something new. Above Whisker Face and Round Lady's mailbox, a shiny balloon is swaying in the warm breeze. When did that get here?

We wait impatiently until the door opens and Whisker Face appears. His dark, furry cheeks are wide and grinning. He brings a finger to his lips. "Shhh," he says.

Grinning right back, Fetch Man slaps his shoulder, while Food Lady wraps him in a hug. Surging with pride, Hattie lifts the cage into Whisker Face's welcoming hands. "Thanks," he says, his grateful eyes smiling.

"Hey, I'm here, too!" I bark, nuzzling Whisker Face's bare feet.

Hattie must be jealous, because she scoops me into her arms. "Shhh," she whispers.

Whisker Face sets the cage on a table. While the rest of the humans chat in low voices, Food Lady tiptoes off. When she returns, her face is full and smiling. I catch the sweet aroma of tiny baby human.

Whisker Face pulls a flimsy strip of paper from his pocket and offers it to Hattie.

She shakes her head. It must be really rotten, like a piece of fruit, because the more he keeps thrusting it at her, the more she refuses to take it.

Fetch Man and Food Lady look on, impressed.

And then, another amazing thing happens. We go back out the door, but Thumper stays behind. He's really gone this time. I'm a little sad. Almost.

But Hattie doesn't smell sad at all. Fetch Man pats her back as we waltz down the driveway toward the floaty balloon. Hattie is different. Tall and proud. I puff myself up, my tail swinging joyfully.

As we walk/sniff our way back across the street, Hattie chatters at Food Lady and Fetch Man for a Long, Long Time. I hear her say two words that I know: "Angel" and "Zahra." Her tone is a mixture of surrender and shame.

Fetch Man and Food Lady listen, exchanging curious looks. Fetch Man speaks to Hattie in a questioning voice.

Hattie takes in a loud breath. She goes back to chattering. But this time, she sounds sure and strong. She says "Angel" and "Zahra" again. Her voice is hopeful.

The tall humans are clearly impressed. Fetch Man rubs Hattie's bushy hair. Food Lady cocks her head, smiling brightly.

Back at home, we're gathered in the Eating Place with turkey sandwiches and pretzels. When all the food is gone and every crumb on the floor has been scarfed down, Angel's voice calls through the back door. "Hattie?"

She slides the door open, and I race to greet her. "I'm so glad you're here!" I bark, leaping on her legs as she joins the other humans in the Eating Place.

She scratches my neck. "Aw, Fenway," she coos.

Angel reaches into her pocket and whips out the two stiff strips from before. Her face beaming with hope, she offers one to Hattie like it's a treat. "Fenway park?" she asks after a quick glance at Fetch Man and Food Lady.

Yippee! I jump on Angel's legs. We're finally going to the park!

But Hattie doesn't seem like she's up for it. She shakes her head. "Zahra," she says.

Angel's forehead scrunches.

Hattie sucks in a shaky breath. She speaks to Angel

in a voice full of remorse. "Fenway," she says, and my ears perk. "Ript-it," she adds.

Angel's eyebrows arch. But her face immediately falls, clearly disappointed. She gazes down at me, frowning and wagging her finger.

I take a few steps away from the table, my tail drooping. What'd I do?

Hattie chatters at Angel some more, but this time she sounds steady, like she's got a plan. Fetch Man and Food Lady give Hattie nods of approval.

Next thing I know, Angel disappears out the sliding door, then quickly returns carrying her jacket.

She hands it to Hattie and Food Lady. They head upstairs.

CHAPTER 21

The next morning, I'm chasing Hattie down the stairs when we hear loud, happy noises coming from outside. We run to the front door and peer out.

Angel and Zahra, in caps and gloves just like Hattie's, bounce up and down in the driveway next door. Tool Man and Muffin Lady appear. They all pile into the car and zoom up the street.

Hattie smells sad for a moment, but then she smiles and scratches my ears. "Ready?" she says.

"I'm so ready! I'm so ready!" I bark, jumping on her legs.

I chase her into the Lounging Place. Hattie makes a pile with cushions from the couch and hides my squeaky toy behind them. While I sniff it out, she squirts smelly cleaner on the carpet and gives it a vigorous rub. I wave the squeaky toy in front of her face, and she pretends to shoo me away with her towel. I dart one way, then the other, as she laughs and laughs.

Next we go upstairs and play hide-and-seek with the clean clothes and books and toys in Hattie's room until they've all disappeared inside the closet or drawers or on shelves. Then we play chase on the back porch with the broom. It's the Best Day Ever.

And the most delicious! At lunchtime, we head out into the Dog Park. Fetch Man fires up the new barbecue and grills hot dogs. Hattie drops two of them right into my mouth. *Mmmmm!*

After lunch, me and Hattie run around the Dog Park, ready to play some more. The grass is littered with so many small branches and twigs, I hardly know which one to grab for a game of keep-away! But apparently, Hattie has an even better idea.

She snatches the nearest stick and flings it across the Dog Park. "Fetch, Fenway!" she cries.

Wowee! I love to play fetch! I tear after that stick, snatch it up, and race back to Hattie. I gaze up at her happily and drop the stick at her feet.

"Attaboy!" she says, patting my head. Food Lady nods approvingly as Hattie stuffs the stick into a black plastic bag. It's so much fun, Hattie rushes all around the Dog Park, grabbing more sticks and twigs and branches to play with.

For a Long, Long Time, me and Hattie play fetch with stick after stick after stick. When we run out of things to fetch and the bag is full and bulging, Fetch Man hauls it off to the garage.

Next we crowd around the hole under the back fence. Food Lady finds a couple of rocks and shoves them into the hole while I help Hattie dig up a little mound of mud. She packs it around the rocks until the hole is completely covered. Food Lady puts one hand on Hattie's shoulder and rubs my head with the other. She smells awfully proud.

Right when I'm wondering what we're going to play next, I hear jingling sounds through the fence. I run over to the Friend Gate and start pawing. "Great news, Hattie!" I bark. "Our friends are coming!"

The Friend Gate clicks and swings open. Goldie and Patches barrel in, and the sniff-circling begins.

Angel and Zahra burst through, too. They run up to Hattie. Even though the other humans have bare arms, Angel is wearing that jacket again. Her hands on her hips, she twirls in the grass. Hattie and Food Lady murmur admiringly and clap their hands.

"Just look at our precious Angel," Patches says dreamily. "She sure is happy."

175

"Yeah," Goldie says. "Must've been all the snuggles we gave her this morning."

Patches cocks her head. "I hate to disagree, but I'm pretty sure it was that growly game of tug-of-war we played after breakfast."

"You've got a point," Goldie says. "She's got a fierce growl on her, that girl."

"Actually, I meant it was terribly sweet of her to let you win," Patches says in her lovely voice.

I prance from Patches to Goldie and back to Patches again. Hooray! Hooray! "You ladies aren't mad at each other anymore. What happened?"

They exchange sisterly looks, then Goldie sighs. "You're going to make us say it? All right. We owe it all to you, Fenway."

"Huh?"

"We may be different," Goldie says.

"And we may remember things a little differently," Patches adds.

Goldie gives her a playful nudge. "But we're family."

"We both love our Angel. And nothing's more important than making her happy," Patches says, dropping down in the grass.

"Besides," Goldie says. "If you can accept a bunny, anything is possible."

"Wow," I say, romping with glee. "That's amazing."

"Awww, Fenway," Zahra coos. She stoops down to pet me.

I lick her hand. She tastes like popcorn and peanuts.

Zahra laughs, then nuzzles Goldie. Hattie bends down and gives Patches a belly rub.

I bound up to Angel, who caresses my ears. She smells like the exact same popcorn and peanuts that Zahra does. But Angel has extra scents on her. My nose sniffs its way to her pocket. It smells like leather and dirt.

Her face grinning, Angel pulls out a white ball, like the one she and Hattie are always playing with.

Angel presents it to Hattie, and she and Zahra both start speaking at once. "Fenway park!" they both gush.

I snuggle against their legs. From the tone of their voices, it's clear they're not talking about a new plan. They're obviously just appreciating a heroic dog in a very happy Dog Park. Aw, shucks.

Apparently Hattie feels the same way. She sucks in a breath, her eyes wide with joy. "Ahhh!" she cries, taking the ball and clutching it to her chest.

Angel and Zahra gaze at Hattie, beaming. Fetch Man and Food Lady share a proud glance.

Hattie reaches out and hugs Angel and Zahra at the same time. "What?" Hattie cries, stepping back. She grabs Angel's wrist and examines a sparkly bracelet. Hattie's eyebrows arch.

Angel shrugs. She and Zahra exchange a smile.

Hattie laughs.

"Your short human looks awfully happy, too," Patches says. "See, I told you accepting the bunny would work out for the best."

"Yeah, about that," I say. "Funny thing . . . he's gone!"

The ladies gasp. "But you brought him back!" Patches cries.

"Don't tell us he ran away!" Goldie says.

"Nope." I thrust out my chest. "Hattie gave him back to the neighbors. Turns out she didn't want him anymore. Like I said, she loves only me."

Patches looks like she's about to say something but changes her mind when there's a commotion in the vegetable patch. We trot over to check it out.

Food Lady's bent over the wire fence, yelling and pointing. Fetch Man is running alongside the leafy lettuces and snaky cucumber vines with Angel and Zahra, their hands outstretched and grabbing. Hattie snatches Fetch Man's cap right off his head. Squatting down, she waves it over a rip in the wire. "Aha!" she shouts.

We all huddle around Hattie. Her face full of surprise, she reaches into the cap and pulls out . . . a bunny? Whoa! Another one?

Everyone gapes at Hattie and the terrified bunny,

who squeals and kicks his muddy paws like the coward he clearly is. Fetch Man and Food Lady glance down at the vegetable patch. Their eyes widen with realization. "Not Fenway!" they cry. Their faces look kindly and apologetic.

Suddenly, I'm the focus of the humans' attention. I'd like to think I'm the hero here, but this time all I did was watch.

Hattie passes the squirming bunny to Fetch Man, then whisks me into her arms. "Oh, Fenway," she sings. She burrows her face into my fur and sways from side to side. She obviously can't get enough of me.

I sigh with happiness. Hattie loves me more than anything in the world. No matter what happens, I'll never doubt her again. I nuzzle into her chest. I sure hope the ladies are enjoying the show.

Acknowledgments

In the summer of 2011, a dog named Fenway popped into my imagination. Four and a half years later, *Fenway and Hattie* became a real live book. Even though *Fenway and Hattie and the Evil Bunny Gang* came to life in roughly half that time, there are way more people to thank. And way more delicious delights to dish out!

A lifetime supply of treats for my exceptionally passionate agent, Marietta B. Zacker, who sank her teeth into this second Fenway and Hattie book and never let go. And for the rest of the incredible Gallt & Zacker team—Nancy Gallt, Ellen Greenberg, and Erin Casey keep your eyes out for the mail truck. You never know when a wicked surprise is coming your way!

Unending boxes of evil bunny cookies for my wise and talented editor, Susan Kochan, for her brilliant insights, abundant sense of humor, and eternal patience. Her enthusiasm for all things Fenway continually blows me away. My characters truly could not be in better hands.

Heaping helpings of goodies for the rest of the astounding team at G. P. Putnam's Sons Books for Young Readers and the Penguin Young Readers Group, especially Katherine Perkins, for countless hours sniffing through the manuscript, Ryan Thomann, for digging up fresh designs, and Rachel Wease and Catherine Hayden, for unleashing Fenway into the world with gusto. The fact that all of you have already moved on to Bigger Things is clearly not a coincidence. May icky vegetables never touch your plate!

Loads of yummy snacks to the many generous friends who graciously read this story and offered feedback that was helpful beyond measure—Hillary Hall Debaun, Joe Lawlor, Cynthia Levinson, Cheryl Lawton Malone, Theresa Milstein, Judy Mintz, Patrice Sherman, and Donna Woelki. And a special vegan treat for Jeff Garvin, who gave this book its name.

Sweets upon sweets for the gang I'm so lucky to be a member of—the Sweet Sixteens debut middle grade and young adult authors—whose unwavering support and friendship I'd be truly lost without. Sharing the writing journey with these outstanding authors and "best buddies" has been an unbelievable honor.

A whole library of chocolate squirrels for rock-star

teacher and librarian friends of the Nerdy Book Club, particularly those who hungrily embraced *Fenway and Hattie* long before it ever hit the shelves—Margie Myers-Culver, Jason Lewis, Jennifer Kelley Reed, Lesley Burnap, Jana Eschner, Kurt Stroh, and Michele Knott, just to name a few of Fenway's very earliest champions. These educators not only have an insatiable appetite for books themselves but are dedicated to nourishing the next generation of Book Nerds in the classroom and beyond. I am continually impressed and inspired by these friends, as well as every new Nerdy friend I make.

And finally, an all-you-can-eat buffet for my family, who deserves extra rewards every day. Even Kipper.

Join Fenway and Hattie on another adventure! Turn the page for an excerpt from the next book in the series.

Fenway and Hattie

Up to New Tricks*

Victoria J. Coe

CHAPTER 1

I scramble through Hattie's blankets, searching for the used-to-be bear. His legs are long gone. But he's still got an arm and a head with two button eyes. And most important of all, he's always here when I need him—just like Hattie. They're both always up for a loving snuggle or a thrilling game of keep-away.

Which I am about to win.

My expert nose leads me under the pillow . . . *chomp!* Game on!

I leap off the bed and tear around the room. Hattie's hot on my tail, waving a towel. She is the best short human ever, even if she's no match for a Jack Russell Terrier like me.

"Fenway!" she cries.

Ha! I dive behind the chair, my sides barely heaving. There's no way she can get me!

Hattie's bushy head appears. Her face is splattered with the wonderful mud we romped through on our walk. "Fenn-waay," she coaxes, her voice too sweet to be real.

Like I'd fall for that act. She's out to win!

Well, so am I, Hattie!

Her fingers brush my leg, but I'm already on the move. I shoot out onto the rug. I'm headed for the door when—

Whoa! Everything goes black. And there's a towel over my head.

Really, Hattie? Is this the best you've got?

One wiggle, two shakes, and the drape-y towel falls to the floor. Whoopee! I'm free again!

For the moment. I spin around, ready to take off, but find myself nose-to-nose with Hattie. And pinned between her legs.

Her eyes widen in victory. I gaze up at my short human's dirt-smudged face, so happy, so full of love. She's won. I've lost. Game over.

The used-to-be bear falls to the floor. There's only one thing left to do.

I leap into Hattie's outstretched arms. If the game's got to end, it might as well be on my terms. I sigh happily into her wonderful scent of mint and vanilla. And dirt.

"Aw, Fenway," she coos, nuzzling my neck. She sets me on the rug and rubs the towel over my mud-caked fur.

Aaaaah, that's the spot! I roll onto my back, my hind leg kicking with delight.

Hattie wipes my brown paw, then my white paw. A Long Time Ago, I convinced her that towel rubs are way better than baths. For us both! All it took was some kicking and thrashing—and maybe a lot of splashing, too. But what can I say? She learned her lesson well.

Hattie's still toweling me off when Food Lady's voice booms up the stairs.

"Uh-oh." Hattie glances at her own mud-splattered legs. She grabs the dirty towel and rushes into the hall. I follow her as far as the Bathtub Room.

"Uh-oh" is right! From the safety of the doorway, I hear water whooshing into the sink. Pretty soon, white soapy lather coats Hattie's hands and face. Her knees, too.

I wince. Even from here, I can smell her great muddy scent washing away. Then the odor of perfume-y flowers hits my nose. Eeeee-yew! And worse than that, Hattie's got an evil gleam in her eye. And a pile of suds in her hand.

My ears droop with worry. She's not getting any ideas, is she?

Hattie bends over. She purses her lips like she's about to blow those yucky suds at me. "Fenn-waay . . . oh, Fenn-waay," she taunts.

I step back, my hackles raised in alarm. "Oh no, you don't!"

Hattie busts into a fit of giggles. She blows the suds harmlessly into the sink.

I drop down in grateful relief. Of course, it was just a trick. Hattie's always looking out for me. How could I expect anything else?

Food Lady's voice booms up the stairs again. Hattie quickly dries her face and hands and knees. She looks me over, then dashes back to her room.

I spring up and trot after her.

Even though it's not bedtime, she grabs my hairbrush. She scoops me up and hastily brushes my matted fur. "Best buddies, best buddies," she sings.

I croon along, howling my own version of our special song. "Best buddies, best buddies," I yowl.

I climb onto her shoulder as she gives my coat a few last strokes. I'm so content, it takes me a moment to pick up a strange sound drifting in from the window.

Chip-chip-chip!

My ears perk up. I peer into the Dog Park below, searching for signs of trouble.

No squirrel-y intruders scurrying along the fence.

No trespassers clattering up the giant tree in the back or poking their rodent-y faces out of Hattie's little house up in the leafy branches.

The grass is calm and quiet, too. The ball Fetch Man threw for me after lunch is right where I left it. The Friend Gate that leads to the Dog Park next door is shut tight. And Food Lady's vegetable patch is as lush and tangle-y as it was this morning.

I scan the bushes on the other side of the Dog Park. My ears prick up. Even from way up here, I can detect rustling and humming. And wait—what's that? Something dives under a low branch. A little tail?

I try to get a better look, but right then Hattie decides it's time to go. She hurries over to the dresser and sets the brush on top. I shoot out of her arms, chasing her into the hall.

We fly down the stairs toward the smell of hamburgers. Hooray! Hooray! I love hamburgers! My dripping tongue can already taste them.

In the Eating Place, Fetch Man and Food Lady are at the table in their usual spots. I perch beside Hattie's chair, sniffing the delicious hamburger and ear of corn on her plate.

As soon as Hattie sits down, Fetch Man clears his throat. As he speaks, I catch a couple of words that I know—"Nana" and "here."

Nana? Here? My tail swishes with excitement. I love Nana!

Nana's the lady human who came and played with us. Back when we lived in our apartment way up high above the honking cars and snorting buses. She slept with me and Hattie when Fetch Man and Food Lady were gone.

Nana!

I can still taste the yummy treats she gave me. I can see her chasing me in the Dog Park. I can hear her cooing at me in her kind voice.

Ah, Nana! Is she coming again?

Maybe so. Fetch Man says "Nana" a lot of times, his voice energetic and eager, like he can't wait to go outside and play fetch.

Food Lady speaks in a happy voice, too. But she also sounds bossy, like there's a big job to do.

Hattie smiles and nods. She looks happy. But she smells worried.

And she's hardly touching her scrumptious food. Something is wrong. Hattie loves Nana as much as I do. What is she worried about?

As soon as I've munched my yummy kibble and the dishes start clanking in the sink, Hattie heads back upstairs. I'm right on her heels.

When we get to her room, she glances over her

shoulder. She lets out a breath, like she's relieved nobody's there. Is she glad nobody's playing chase with us?

Hattie quietly closes the door. She puts her fingers to her lips, shooting me a look of warning.

Whoa. Something important is about to happen!

I follow her to the closet, where she sinks onto the floor. She rummages through shoes and boots and toys. Reaching way in the back, she digs out a big box and wheels it into the room. She gazes at it, frozen. "Hattie-the-Grrate," she whispers.

I cock my head. I've heard those words before. Only they didn't sound miserable when Nana said them. In Nana's voice, they sounded exciting.

Hattie stares at the box with wide eyes, like it's a bone she dug up. But she doesn't smell happy.

My tail rises with curiosity. My nose gets busy sniffing. That box's scent is awfully interesting. And familiar somehow. Is Hattie worried about what's inside this box?

Chapter 2

Cross-legged on the floor, Hattie stares
at the box while I give it a thorough sniffing. Its scents
are old and new at the same time. And also like metal
and plastic. It's a cube, at least twice as tall as me, with
wheels on the bottom. The sides are black, and the
edges are shiny and metallic. The lid has hinges on one
end and a buckle on the other. It's not like any box I've
ever met. Talk about intriguing!

What was this box doing in the back of Hattie's
closet? And more importantly, what is it?

Hattie's face scrunches. She doesn't seem to know
what to do with this box.

So why'd she take it out of the closet?

I can't stand the suspense. I leap into her lap. "Great

news, Hattie!" I bark. "That box could have something wonderful inside. Like sausages! Let's open it!"

"Shhh," she says, frowning, like opening the box is the last thing she wants to do. But she clearly wants me to be happy, because she fiddles with the buckle and lifts the lid—*creeeak!*

My tail thumps with anticipation. I stretch way up, pawing the box, my nose sniffing feverishly. The smells are tantalizing! I need to see what's inside!

I spring onto the chair and peer down into the box. Wowee! My eyes don't know where to look first.

Hattie starts rummaging through silky cloth . . . a tall hat . . . a bunch of fake flowers . . . and she's not acting the least bit surprised. This stuff must be what she was expecting to find.

Hattie digs deeper and pulls out a flow-y cape, a skinny black stick, and a clear plastic box with a rattle-y ball inside.

I fly off the chair to investigate the growing pile of stuff on the floor. Everything smells new, like toys that haven't been played with. Yet at the same time, their aroma is awfully familiar.

The scents take me back to a lovely memory. Nana at our apartment with a box like this one. Nana in the flow-y cape, tapping the tall hat with the stick. Nana's fist, holding fake flowers.

Every sniff reminds me of that wonderful time. Hattie gaping in astonishment. Hattie clapping and cheering. Hattie clinging to Nana's side, full of admiration.

And best of all, I remember me and Nana playing tug-of-war with those silky scarves!

Sniff . . . sniff . . . licorice, coffee, just the right amount of cherry—*Nana!* This box smells like Nana!

It's definitely the same one she brought. Why didn't she take it when she left? And why haven't we seen it until now?

Hattie continues emptying the box, tossing metal rings and silky scarves onto the floor. My nose can hardly keep up with all the amazing things to smell.

Hattie waves the skinny stick through the air. She gazes at it, her eyes wide and full of wonder. It doesn't look like a stick from the ground. I scamper over for a better sniff.

But as soon as I get close, Hattie whisks it out of my reach. She plucks a scarf off the floor and stuffs one end into her fist, the rest of it snaking across the floor.

My tail twirls with excitement. I want that stick, but who can resist a game of tug-of-war? Especially with a silky scarf that's long and oh-so-bitable!

Chomp! My teeth sink into one end of the scarf. I dig in my hind legs and pull, tugging with all my might . . .

And whoa! I skid and stumble backward, crashing

into the chair. The scarf flies out of Hattie's hand, puddling in front of me.

"FEN-way!" Hattie frowns, waggling the stick. "Drop it!"

I unclench my jaws, my end of the scarf falling to the floor. It's pretty clear why she's unhappy. That game of tug-of-war was no fun at all. But only because she didn't even try.

She grabs the scarf, then shoots me a stern look. "Wait," she commands.

I plop down on my bum, tilting my head expectantly. She probably wants to play another game. I sure hope treats are involved!

Hattie makes another fist and once again starts stuffing the scarf inside her hand. She pokes and pokes until it completely disappears. "Watch," she says, tapping her fist with the stick.

An invitation if ever I saw one! I romp onto her knee, my jaws ready to nab that stick.

"Ab-ra-ca—no!" Hattie shouts. "Fenway, stay!" She waves it out of my reach.

"No fair!" I back into her arm, and the silky scarf slides out of her hand. Aha! I sink my teeth into it, but before I can take off, Hattie grabs me by the collar.

"FEN-way," she scolds.

I let the scarf drop. "What's the matter?" I bark. "Don't you want to play?"

She picks up the slobbery scarf, her eyes bulging as she studies tiny rips in the fabric. With a loud sigh, she hangs her head and tosses the stick onto the floor. "Hattie-the-Grrate," she mutters, sounding miserable.

I nuzzle against her leg. "Don't worry, Hattie. We can play some other game."

She lifts me into a hug. What can I say? Hattie's always up for snuggling—hey!

Plop! Suddenly, I'm inside the Nana-box. *Thud!* The lid shuts and I'm plunged into blackness. And trapped!

I paw furiously at the box. "What's the meaning of this?" I yelp. I jump as high as I can, but the lid won't budge.

I fall back down. Yikes! This box is dark and lonely. And scary. Clearly, the Nana-box is no place for a dog. I have to escape!

"Hattie, help!" I whine. "I'm stuck and I can't get out!" Isn't Hattie right outside the box? Why isn't she rescuing me?

She would help if she could. Maybe she can't hear me. I bark louder. "Get me out of here!" I'm about to try leaping again, when I hear a curious sound. I cock my head and concentrate.

"Shhhhh!"

Is that Hattie? Who is she shushing? It couldn't be me. I'm the one she needs to hear!

Tap! Tap! Tap!

I listen some more.

"Ab-ra-ca-dab-ra!"

Hattie's voice! She *is* right outside. I knew she'd come save me! "Hattie, it's me! Help! I'm in the box!" I scratch with all my might.

Snap! The buckle opens. *Creeeak!* The lid lifts up. Whew! It worked! She finally heard me!

I leap into her loving arms. The best place to be!

Panting with wild relief, I slobber her cheeks. "Thank you . . . Hattie . . . I knew you'd . . . come through!"

"Aw, Fenway," she sighs, patting my head. Clearly, she feels bad for my suffering. More than anything else, she wants me to be happy.

As the sky gets dark, we climb into bed. I go to wrap my paw around the used-to-be bear when I notice something curious. One of his button eyes has vanished. What could've happened to it?

Get a dog's-eye view of the world in this enthusiastic "tail" about two best friends!

Fenway and his beloved short human, Hattie, are the perfect pair. She loves romping in the Dog Park, playing fetch, and eating delicious snacks as much as he does. But when they move from the city to the suburbs, there are big changes. Hattie hangs out in a squirrely tree house and plays ball without him. Crushed and confused, Fenway sets out on a mission. He's going to get his Hattie back and nothing will stop him—not the Wicked Floor, not the dreaded Gate, not even a giant squirrel!